A Temporary Boyfriend

The Fake Love Series - Book 2

Summer Dowell

To Quin.
Who told me I don't need to dedicate any more
books to him but I'm not a quitter.

Table of Contents

Chapter 1   8

Chapter 2   16

Chapter 3   29

Chapter 4   37

Chapter 5   53

Chapter 6   61

Chapter 7   82

Chapter 8   96

Chapter 9   113

Chapter 10   134

Chapter 11   144

Chapter 12   165

Chapter 13   **181**

Chapter 14   **194**

Chapter 15   **212**

Chapter 1

"Ms. Hudson?"

The receptionist's monotone did nothing to calm Madison's nerves. Nerves that were soaring to the levels of a high school boy about to ask a girl to prom.

"Y-yes! That's me." Madison fought to keep the shrill out of her voice. "I'm here to see Mr. Stevens?"

As the older woman peered over her reading glasses, Madison shifted her weight, slightly regretting the utterly chic but slightly precarious high heels she'd chosen to wear. She hoped she wouldn't trip.

After glancing at her computer screen one more time, the emotionless receptionist nodded. "Yes, he's expecting you." She stood and simply said, "Follow me."

Madison trailed the slight woman down a hallway, each side lined by heavy, imposing-looking office doors. She finally paused before the slightly ajar one at the end. "He's in there. Feel free to walk in." With that, she turned and headed back toward her desk.

Well, not the warmest welcome she had ever received—she was pretty sure her grocery store clerk had more charisma than that—but Madison didn't have energy to brood on it. Taking a deep breath, she turned toward her future. Time to focus. Should she knock first? The woman had said Mr. Stevens was expecting her, but she didn't want to seem presumptuous.

After a moment of ridiculous indecision, she tapped lightly on the door. Immediately, she was rewarded with a loud "Come in" from the other side.

Stepping into the room, the sight of a large man seated at an equally large desk greeted her. Mr. Stevens. CEO of Sube Nutritionals, one of the leading vitamin and supplement brands in the world. He was studying something on the oversized computer screen in front of him.

When he finally glanced at her, still hovering by the door, he stood. "Come in, come in." He motioned with his arm. "I am just reviewing a memo."

Madison wiped her palms on the back of her suit pants and stepped forward, desperately trying to leave her nerves behind. "Mr. Stevens," she said, reaching out with her hand, "it's an honor to meet you."

He leaned across the desk, and his large fingers enveloped hers. "Yes, Ms. Hudson, so glad to have you in today. And feel free to call me Dave. I leave the Mr. Stevens stuff for my clients." He said this last part with a grin, a row of white teeth reflecting back at her.

The fact that he knew her name gave Madison a boost of confidence. She needed to relax; this was just another interview. The fact that it was with the CEO of her dream company meant nothing.

He motioned toward one of the chairs in front of his desk. "Please, have a seat."

Dave settled himself back into his own as Madison eased into one of the leather armchairs. The material felt like butter as she ran her hand along the arm, a sure sign of its quality and, subsequently, the pretty penny it had cost.

"So, Ms. Hudson, tell me a little bit about yourself."

"Please, call me Madison." She would milk this first-name basis for all it was worth. She crossed her ankles and tucked them behind one leg of the chair. "Well, I recently graduated from Colorado State University with a Masters in Nutritional Science." Madison rattled off some more of her basic credentials. She was one of the top of her class, graduating with full honors and a 4.0 GPA. She'd spent the last two years in a research internship at the state's public health offices. All the usual stuff that impressed employers.

After another minute, Dave cut her off. "This is all great. I can tell you're well qualified for the position, Madison. If you weren't, you wouldn't be sitting in my office today."

Madison tried to force a smile, but the fact that he wasn't eating up her experience made her grip the armchair with a little more force than necessary.

"There's a reason I only get involved in the last round of these interviews. I let my colleagues deal with narrowing it down to the top candidates." He smiled and leaned back in his chair. "What I'm saying is, I know you're *qualified* for the position. What I want to know is if you'll be a good fit for this company. We are a team here. I want to make sure I have employees that mesh well together." He interlocked his fingers in demonstration. "So I want to know more about *you*. Tell me who Madison Hudson is."

Madison swallowed and tried to ignore the bead of moisture now running down her back. She said a prayer of thanks that she'd decided to wear a suit jacket—one that was doing its part to hide any sweat marks. These were the kinds of questions she dreaded. She'd rather talk about R&D standard operating procedures or ingredient documentation and proofs. She didn't want to talk about herself. What was there really to tell?

"Well, I'm your average girl," she began, looking to him for clues about what he was digging for. "I enjoy being in nature. Specifically, I love bike riding. I feel like it's something I can always pick up and do no matter where I am."

Dave watched her, giving no indication as to his feelings. Clearly, the outdoors wasn't his thing.

"Um...what else...I love animals…" Everybody loved animals, right? Maybe this guy was a member of PETA or something. "My current apartment doesn't allow pets, but I plan to get a dog one day."

No reaction from him.

She began twirling her hair subconsciously. What did he want to hear? "I also love cooking. I guess you could say that's how I got started in food science. As a kid, I was always in the kitchen. My mom used to say I would use up all her ingredients before she ever got to them."

At the mention of her family, a smile crept across his face. "Oh yeah? Tell me about your family."

A spark of hope raced through her at his sudden interest. "I'm the youngest of three children. I have two older brothers, which left very few dull moments in our house."

Dave let out a hearty laugh. "I can imagine. I have three boys myself. So, tell me, is family important to you?"

Madison nodded her head in jerky motions. Clearly, she'd found a winning topic with this guy. "Yes! My family and I are all very close. I can't wait to have one of my own soon." Okay, maybe that pushed the truth a little. Madison did hope to have a family one day, but she didn't plan to start childbearing anytime soon. A husband usually came first. And a boyfriend before that.

Dave tapped the desk with his pen—a very heavyset, gold-tipped pen that Madison assumed hadn't come from a massive multi-pack from Walmart. "That's wonderful. We're a very family-oriented company. So, you must be in a relationship yourself, then, if you're contemplating children?"

Somehow, she found herself nodding. "Yes, m-my boyfriend and I often talk about our future family." Madison suddenly felt like she was in the middle of an out-of-body experience. Had she really just said that? She wasn't dating anyone. And she definitely didn't have a boyfriend she talked about having children with.

"That's wonderful. Family is one of the most important things in life." Dave beamed at her. "It took me longer than I like to realize that myself, but I can say nothing—not even this company—comes before my wife and kids."

Madison nodded like a puppet on a string. "Yes, I can't imagine anything else coming before them. I'm sure I'll feel the same way soon." Only the ache of her pinched toes made her accept she wasn't dreaming. She really was sitting here discussing her soon-to-be imaginary family with her potential boss. Almost subconsciously, she perched on the edge of her seat, as if waiting for him to call her out as a liar.

Fortunately, or maybe unfortunately, he did nothing of the sort. "We're looking for people just like you. Those who are steady and have a plan for life. Hopefully, one that includes settling with us." He said this last part with a wink.

Madison tried to ignore the queasiness in her stomach. "Oh yeah, that's what Ethan—my boyfriend—always says. If we don't start planning now, it'll never happen."

Stop, stop, stop! her mind raged silently, but she couldn't. She tried to smile to cover up her inner turmoil and prayed it didn't come off as a grimace.

"Ethan sounds like a smart man. This is all great, really great." Dave was back to leaning forward, excitement in his eyes. "Well, I think we've done enough background chatting. Let's talk about this job for a little bit."

Madison said a silent prayer of thanks that he didn't give her time to describe the imaginary, four-bedroom house in the suburbs they were in escrow on or the names they'd picked out for their three future children.

The next fifteen minutes were actually a total blur for Madison. She was pretty sure Dave spent the bulk of the time explaining the position and expectations, but all she could think about was the lie she had told him. Why had she said all that about a fake boyfriend? She blamed her nerves. She had a tendency to ramble when things got awkward.

By the time the interview wound down, she resolved that if she did get the job, she would just casually mention that she and her boyfriend had actually broken up. That way, there would be no chance of anyone asking to meet him.

"Well, Madison, I have to say I am pleased with what I've seen today," Dave said as they made their way to his door.

Her spirits soared at his words. Yes, she may have spilled a few white lies during their discussion, but that would all be water under the bridge in a week or so.

"As a matter of fact, our company is hosting a dinner this Saturday," he continued. "It's actually a fundraiser for a humanitarian project we're running down in Mexico." He waved his hand as if swatting away a fly. "Not that that matters. But I want you to come. It will be good for you to meet everyone and get a feel for the company dynamics."

This had to be a good thing, right? She doubted he would invite every person he interviewed to this dinner. Had she gotten the position?

Before she could gush her thanks, he added, "And bring Ethan with you. We'll all want to meet him, too."

And just like that, her soaring spirits crash landed.

"Oh, are—are you sure? I would hate to inconvenience anyone, especially at such late notice—"

"Not at all. Like I said, we are a tight-knit group. You work for us, you become like family. I can't wait to meet him."

Dave had opened the door by this point. Madison could have continued protesting, but she didn't think it would have mattered. He clearly didn't become a CEO by being a pushover.

"Well, thank you. I—I mean, *we*—will be delighted to come this weekend." She shook his hand again; this time her nerves piled up for an entirely different reason.

"Wonderful. Talk to Jill at the front desk. She'll give you all the details about the dinner. We'll chat again then."

With a nod, he turned on his heel, leaving Madison staring down the foreboding hallway, wondering what she had just gotten herself into.

Chapter 2

Eric leaned his head against the metal post next to him. He made one more attempt to find a comfortable position in the hard plastic chair before giving up. It was going to be a long night.

He sat in front of Gate 58 at the LAX airport. At some point, he would need to make his way to Gate 55, where his flight had been rescheduled, but he had about four hours to walk the three hundred yards, so he was in no rush.

The airplane he was supposed to be on had an engine malfunction, and now they were in the process of finding a replacement plane. Apparently, they didn't have a bunch of those laying around.

Eric sighed, a quiet protest against the unfairness of the airline systems. Although, realistically, he couldn't complain. It wasn't like he had anywhere he urgently needed to be. This was the beginning of a two-week break in between jobs, and the only reason he was flying to Colorado was because that was where his storage unit was.

Eric used to keep an actual apartment in Denver. He liked to think of it as his home base. The place he could relax in between clients. But his work schedule had gotten demanding enough that it was pointless to pay rent on an apartment he was never in. Instead, he cancelled his lease and moved the remaining items he didn't want to sell to a storage unit nearby.

As such, when he did get a rare break from work, he simply stayed in a local hotel until he started another contract.

It wasn't an ideal life. Although, the daily room cleaning and pillow fluffing wasn't such a bad perk. But despite the fact that people would hate the constant moving, Eric had gotten used to it.

His phone vibrated, and he looked down to read the notice.

Player ChessBoss231 has moved knight to h4.

Eric opened the online chess game and studied the board. ChessBoss231 had turned out to be a pretty good player. However, his last move freed up one of his bishops, and it would come back to bite him. Eric slid his queen over four squares then turned his phone off again.

He drummed his fingers on his leg.

He could call someone.

He hadn't talked to either of his parents in a while. Or he could call his sister, April. She'd probably appreciate knowing he was in town, seeing as she lived in Denver herself.

April and he had grown up pretty close since there was only the two of them. His parents always claimed they were afraid to have any more children because then they'd be outnumbered. He grinned to himself. Neither he nor April were exactly mellow kids, so it had probably been a smart move.

Yeah, he should let her know he would be around this next week, but Eric couldn't bring himself to dial her number just then.

"Hi, is this seat taken?"

He looked up to see a tall blonde with legs a mile long standing over him. Despite the rather empty terminal, she seemed intent on sitting next to him.

"It is now," he said with a grin and motioned for her to sit as he straightened in his own seat.

Sometimes, not being tied down was a blessing.

*****

"Deep breaths, Madison. Slow, deep breaths. Now, tell me again—this time in English preferably—what happened?"

Madison's roommate, April, sat on the oak coffee table in front of her. Madison herself was sunk deep into the middle of the sofa they'd inherited from her grandma. The suede couch had a strong lavender smell that was currently saturating her sense of smell.

"I told you. I informed my potential boss that I am in a committed relationship with a man named Ethan today. A man I plan on soon having children with," she said, her voice becoming more shrill with each word. "And now"—she threw her head back—"my potential boss wants to meet this imaginary Ethan at a dinner on Saturday." It sounded even more ridiculous when she said it out loud.

April brought her knees up to her chest and rested her chin on them, covering her mouth. "You're talking about the interview you had today, right?" she asked, her words slightly muffled.

"Yessss," Madison groaned. "And stop laughing; I can see your smile. Getting a dream job like this is the whole reason I went to grad school. It is the perfect opportunity that will probably never come up again in my life!" She let out another groan.

"Whoa, sister, let's go back to those deep breaths again," April said, lowering her legs since they'd clearly failed in hiding her laughter. "So, let me get this straight. You told your boss about an imaginary boyfriend named Ethan that you're planning on repopulating the Earth with?" She was working hard to keep her lips together instead of letting them spread into a wide grin. "Can I ask how the heck this came up in a job interview?"

"I don't know, I was trying to impress him?"

"How is having a boyfriend going to impress your boss? I thought these guys worked in nutrition, not matchmaking."

Madison dropped her face into her hands, not sure if she wanted to laugh right along with April or cry. "He seemed so happy when I mentioned wanting to have kids one day. You know me, the second I get nervous, I start rambling whatever comes to my head." Her voice was now the muffled one as she talked into her palms. "I figured, if he thought I was in a committed relationship, he'd see me as a reliable employee."

"Don't you think he's going to question your reliability—not to mention your mental stability—when he finds out you made the whole thing up?"

Sometimes April's bluntness was hard to take.

"If you haven't gathered, I clearly wasn't thinking straight during this whole interview," Madison said, shimmying deeper into the couch.

Her roommate studied her for a second before grabbing her phone. "Okay, it's fine. Really, this will be fine. I, your amazingly generous best friend, will help pull you through this one."

Madison narrowed her eyes, suspicious at April's suddenly perky tone.

"We'll simply have to come up with a short-term boyfriend for the weekend." April shrugged, folding her legs into a cross-legged position. "Just to help you get the job. That shouldn't be too hard. I'm sure we can find *someone* to play the role."

Madison wasn't sure she liked the way that word *someone* sounded. "Whoa, before you go calling every male we know, remember, this has to be someone remote. Someone I don't normally associate with. I'm planning on breaking up with this 'boyfriend' by next week." She used air quotes to emphasize the title.

"Got it. We're looking for a guy that no one in your work will have any reason to see after this dinner."

"Ideally, I'd like him to have a good set of social skills as well," Madison added. "Not to be picky, but he's going to be a reflection on me. So, it would be nice if he could hold a normal conversation with the other guests."

"Any other requests?" her friend asked dryly.

Madison shrugged. "I mean, I wouldn't be upset if he happened to look like a male model either. I'm partial to the tall, dark, and handsome type. But I can deal with a blond for one night."

April rolled her eyes and continued scrolling through her phone.

Madison grinned, feeling slightly more hopeful than she had all afternoon. Maybe April was right. All she had to do was find a guy for one night. That couldn't be too hard, could it?

Unfortunately, April was looking less confident by the minute. "Hmm...just give me a second..."

The longer the silence stretched, the more Madison's momentary hope sunk. "There's no one, is there? I mean, honestly, who am I going to find to be my pretend boyfriend by Saturday?" She stretched out, face down, on the couch, inhaling the calming lavender like it was a lifeline. How could she have gotten herself into this mess?

"I mean, there's always Jake," April offered.

"I am not asking my ex-boyfriend to pretend to be my current boyfriend," Madison muttered into the cushion. "We probably wouldn't make it through the cocktail hour without being at each other's throats."

"Well, if you're going to be *particular*," April grumbled, still scrolling.

Madison didn't even acknowledge the comment. Instead, she started considering all the ways she could get out of Saturday evening's dinner. She could pretend to be sick. Or maybe a sudden family emergency could take her out of town.

"How about Pete next door?"

She lifted her head. "No. One hundred percent no. And why do you have Pete's number in your phone?"

April shrugged. "I don't know. I think he gave it to me in case of an emergency."

Pete was their hermit of a neighbor who happened to have an obsession with Madison. He asked her out basically every time he saw her. She had learned to avoid walking past his door whenever possible.

"Maybe you could get one of your brothers to do it."

Madison smacked the edge of the couch. "Wow, you somehow managed to come up with a worse option than Pete. I wouldn't have thought it was possible."

Throwing her hand in the air, April gave a long sigh. "Well, I don't see you offering up any names."

"That's because I've already given up," Madison moaned. "Why don't I just come clean to Dave? Explain it was a simple misunderstanding."

"He misunderstood you when you said you are in a serious relationship with a man named Ethan, the father of your future offspring? A man you are bringing to a work dinner this Saturday night?" April's monotone voice gave her her answer.

"Fine. I'll just put in my resignation. I'll be the first person to resign from a job before they even had it."

Just then, April's phone buzzed. She glanced at it for a second before tossing it on the coffee table. As soon as the case hit the wood, though, she grabbed it again. "Wait a second, I've got it!"

"Got what?" Madison asked with little interest as she pulled out her own phone. "Do you feel like a pizza? I think a dose of cheese might make me feel bett—"

"Madison, I've got the perfect guy for you."

Madison pushed herself up to her elbows. "You do? Who?"

"My brother."

"*Your* brother? The computer programmer? The one you insist is a complete nerd who could never land a girl if his life depended on it?"

"Yes! His name's Eric." April's huge smile showed she wasn't understanding Madison's dismay.

"I thought your brother traveled all the time. How in the world are you going to get him to fly in for the weekend to go to a dinner with me?" Madison had gone back to her pizza order on her phone. "Do you feel like pepperoni or sausage?"

April grabbed the device out of her roommate's hands. "Because..." she answered, drawing out the word, "he's already going to be in town anyway." She waved her phone in Madison's face. "He just texted me that he's flying in this weekend. It's foolproof."

"I don't know...won't he be busy?" Madison's gut still wasn't on board with this plan.

"No, he's got a break between jobs for a couple weeks. And don't worry, his social life is basically null, so he'll definitely be free." April narrowed her eyes at her friend. "You two will be perfect," she whispered almost to herself.

Madison missed April's last comment. "Are you sure he can play the part and everything?" she asked, chewing on her lip.

Her roomate stood and put her hands on her hips. "Look, missy, two seconds ago you were begging for anyone.

Don't get all high-handed now that I've found you an answer."

Madison lifted her hands in surrender. "Alright, alright, you're right. Yes, you're right. Thank you for offering your somewhat geeky brother to be my fake boyfriend. I appreciate it more than you can imagine." She grinned when April nodded her acceptance of the halfhearted apology. "My question is, are you sure he'll do it?"

"Of course. Eric would do anything for me."

*****

"No."

"Ah, come on, Eric. You can't say no to this. We need you!"

"No, April, I'm not playing Prince Charming to your little roommate. Go find some other sucker for your weird girl plans."

"Clearly, I'm not asking you to play Prince Charming, since I know that's a role you could never fill." April's reply was sharp even over the phone. "And this is not a weird girl plan. Madison just had a little misunderstanding during her job interview and would greatly appreciate it if you could pretend to be her boyfriend for a night." April paused, letting the words sink in. "It's not that big of a deal. Plus, you'll get a free dinner out of it."

Eric rolled his eyes as he leaned against the empty baggage cart—the one that was at least fifteen minutes late getting his flight's luggage out. "I can afford to pay for food, April. I'm not exactly struggling financially."

"I know, you are just *so* successful and independently wealthy that there's no way you could help your little sister—your only sibling and blood relative that matters—for one night."

April's ridiculousness got a grin out of him. "Sorry, sis, I've got my weekend filled. I wish I could help you, but I just can't."

She spent another ten minutes protesting, but Eric remained firm. The last thing he wanted to do was get involved in some sort of drama. After hanging up, he checked the baggage claim screen one more time. Carousel four should be shooting out his luggage any second now. He sighed and decided he might as well book his hotel for the next two weeks. It was something he usually took care of in advance, but time had gotten away from him last week at work.

Ten minutes later, he stared, dumbfounded, at his phone. There were no availabilities. None. Zip. Every place he called was booked solid. At first, he'd been confused, but when one desk clerk reminded him about the NFL playoffs this week, it all fell into place.

Of course everything was booked. The Denver Broncos were in the third round of the playoffs against the Dallas Cowboys this weekend. No wonder there were no vacancies anywhere.

Eric considered his options. His next job was in Boston in two weeks. He could probably fly out early and find a hotel there. However, that would entail a bunch of flight rescheduling, and Boston hotel prices were at least double what they were here in Denver. Economically, it wouldn't make sense.

Plus, Denver was home. He wanted to relax here during his time off.

Suddenly, a thought hit him. He could stay with his sister. Normally, he wouldn't try to bum off family, but his conscience was still hitting him for refusing to help her. Maybe they could make some sort of trade. He'd pretend to be her roommate's boyfriend for a night, if they let him sleep on their couch for a week.

Logically, it made sense. The hard thing would be calling April and eating his words.

Eric sighed and searched for her name in his recent calls. As expected, she picked up after the first ring.

"Yes, brother-who-is-apparently-too-important-for-family-now?"

"Hey, April, so I've been thinking about your request." He ran one hand through his dark hair, praying he wouldn't regret his next words. "I've been thinking you were right, and I should help my little sister and her roommate out in their time of need."

He could hear April sniff into the phone. "What makes you think we still need you? Maybe we've found someone better."

Eric rolled his eyes. "Well, considering you called me less than ten minutes ago, I'd be pretty surprised if that were the case."

April's voice got muffled for a minute, like she was talking to someone else—probably the roommate in need. Eric figured he better put in his stipulation for room-and-board before they decided.

"I do have one request, though, if I do this for you," he added loudly, mouthing "sorry" when a mother holding a sleeping baby gave him a hard look.

April's voice came back clear again. "Okay, what?"

He moved away from the baggage carousel and the offended mother before answering. "Can I stay at your guys' place for the next week?"

There was silence on the other end. "Well yeah, sure, that should be fine." She paused before adding, "*Are* you having financial troubles, Eric? I can totally help out if you are. I didn't mean what I said earlier about you being independently wealthy or anything—"

"No, no, I'm totally fine, April," Eric cut in, noticing the baggage cart beginning to spin. "It's just that I didn't make a hotel reservation, and everywhere is booked because of the playoffs this weekend."

"Oh, so *this* is why you changed your mind." April's voice got a sassy tone now. "You actually need us."

Eric sighed as he began walking back toward the moving carousel. "Let's call it a fair trade. I just landed, so I'll probably be to your place in about an hour. Is that okay?"

April's voice hadn't lost its glee. "Yep, see you in a bit, bro."

Eric slid the phone into his pocket, his eyes on the lineup of black suitcases already streaming down the runway. He hoped his sister's roommate wasn't totally weird or antisocial. Or worse yet, that she was the clingy, emotional type. Another dozen worst-case scenarios ran through his head, each of them more pitiful than the last.

He was already beginning to regret his decision.

Chapter 3

Madison owed April big. Sure, her brother was bound to be a computer geek, and Saturday would likely be an awkward night, but at least Madison could save face at her future job.

Her *potential* future job.

Madison had to keep reminding herself that she didn't have the position yet. Dave had just been so reassuring at her interview. She felt like he had basically handed her the contract. But she knew counting her chickens before they hatched would just cause trouble.

She sighed as she pulled out the spare comforter and sheets from their linen closet. April had an extra pillow or two, so with their powers combined, they could scramble up enough bedding for Eric to sleep on the couch for the next week.

Carrying her load into the living room, Madison set them on the ground next to the coffee table. April walked back in with a spare pillow as well.

"So, tell me again about your brother," Madison said as she scanned the carpet. It could probably do with a good vacuuming if they were going to have a guest. Not that she was sure if April's brother counted as a guest. He was, technically, family.

"Eric? Haven't I told you about him before?" April asked. She snuggled her way into one corner of the couch.

"Just that he's a computer whiz that works all the time." Madison's clean-freak side won out, and she pulled the vacuum out of the hallway closet.

"Well, you know basically everything about him then," April said with a grin.

"Come on. You've got to give me more than that. Tell me some details. He is supposed to be my boyfriend, after all. I should probably know a little more about him other than he's a geek."

"Well, let's see, he loves computers and everything to do with technology. I wouldn't say he's super into sports or anything, but he does like outdoorsy stuff like hiking." April scrunched up her nose. "He actually has this weird love of camping. I don't know who in their right mind would ever purposely sleep on the ground."

Madison listened as she unwound the vacuum cord.

"He loves chess, too..." April continued, tapping her chin, "...I don't know. I can't think of much else."

Madison gave her the side eye. "You've never really said much about his appearance. Is he cute?"

April suddenly seemed very interested in her fingernails. "He's all right. Eric's never been a ladies man. He was always too obsessed with his gadgets growing up. He's not bad to look at, though."

Her roommate's vague answer confused Madison, but she let the subject drop. "Well, what I don't know about him I can always make up. We just need to fake this for one night."

April grinned at her. "We'll see what happens."

Madison was about to ask what she meant, but instead, she plugged in the vacuum and got to work.

*****

An hour later, Madison was sitting in her room when she heard a knock. It must have been April's brother. She contemplated doing herself up a bit. She was, after all, asking this guy to be her fake boyfriend. She probably should look somewhat appealing.

April's description of him left her with a half-hearted effort, however. Her old jeans and messy bun would have to do.

She heard April squeal, and surprise hit her when a deep voice answered. For some reason, she had imagined April's brother as a scrawny guy with a high-pitched, squeaky voice. Thick rimmed glasses and a solid, middle hair part rounded out the image.

But the mature tone that echoed through the house was anything but squeaky.

Madison scurried to her bedroom door and opened it a crack. She couldn't see anything from her angle.

Taking a deep breath, she rolled her shoulders back. She needed to approach this with confidence. This was nothing more than a business transaction. The fact that she was asking a total stranger to be her boyfriend for a night was nothing to be ashamed of.

She turned the corner with what she hoped was a matter-of-fact air.

The back of his head was the first thing she saw. His frame immediately struck her. He didn't have the build she had expected. He had to be easily over six feet tall, and his broad shoulders spoke of someone who visited the gym regularly, not just the computer lab.

April noticed Madison's entrance over her brother's shoulder. Obviously noting his sister's movement, the man turned to look at Madison.

And that was when things froze.

The first thought in Madison's head was that she couldn't believe she had no makeup on. Not even mascara to give a boost to her poor excuse for eyelashes.

The second was that she was going to kill April.

April's brother, Eric, was not just "all right" as she had said. He was drop dead gorgeous.

His ashy black hair stood out in stark contrast to his light blue eyes. The kind of blue that matched the sky right after it rained. His hollow cheeks were lined with a faint hint of stubble, and his jawline ended in a mouth quirked in a half smile.

"You must be my girlfriend," he said in the same deep voice she'd heard moments before.

For the life of her, Madison couldn't come up with a single word in response.

April tried to smooth over the moment by grabbing her brother's arm, turning him back to her. "You be nice about this, Eric. We're doing you as much of a favor by letting you stay here as you are for us." As she said this, she glanced at Madison with lifted eyebrows.

The momentary distraction brought Madison to her senses.

"Yes! I am that girlfriend," she said, shifting Eric's attention back to her. But the second those blue eyes landed on her face, she began to stutter again. "I—that is—thank you for helping me. I know it's kind of an...unusual request." If he could just stop staring at her like that, she could think clearly.

"No, it's cool. I get people asking me to be their fake boyfriend all the time."

He said this with such a straight face Madison didn't know if he was joking.

"Oh...well then..."

His mouth cracked slightly. "I'm kidding. You're the first." He bent down and picked up the suitcase he'd set on the floor. "But who knows, if this goes well, maybe I can turn it into a side gig for myself."

"Will you stop," April exclaimed from behind him. "Move it, I'll show you your living quarters for the next week."

As they shuffled by her, Madison shook her head. She didn't know why she was being so weird. She had two brothers of her own. She knew Eric was just messing with her.

"Here is your bedroom," she heard April say from the living room.

As she walked into the room herself, she saw Eric standing with his hands on his hips. "Where's the mint on my pillow?" he questioned.

April threw the offending pillow at him. "This is a self-service hotel. There will be no laundry or continental breakfast," she said as she eased down to the floor. "However, we do provide free cable and WiFi."

"What about a pool?"

Madison couldn't hold back a snicker this time. Eric turned an appreciative glance her way.

"So, how has work been? Where was your last project?" April asked.

While April and Eric caught up, Madison considered her options. She really wanted to go back to her room and spend the next thirty minutes fixing her hair and makeup. But that would be ridiculous. He'd already seen her, anyway, right? She resigned herself to her current appearance, trying to casually comb back the highlighted flyaways that had escaped her bun. Giving up on the attempt, she joined the siblings in their conversation.

Eric had seated himself on the far side of the couch, and April had taken up the center of the floor. That just left the other side of the couch for Madison. She slid down onto the empty cushion, hoping the perpetual wafts of lavender would calm her tension at sitting next to the most attractive geek she'd ever encountered.

"So, why are you still teaching the Zumba classes if you hate them?"

They had obviously moved on from Eric's work to discussing April's career as a fitness instructor.

"Because there's no one else to take the shifts, and they pay me time and a half right now." April shrugged. "By next month, they should have another instructor, and I'll go back to normal hours."

Eric looked at Madison during the break in their conversation. Was that intrigue she saw in his eyes? Or just plain curiosity? She didn't have anything on her face, did she?

"So, it's Madison, right? I guess we were never formally introduced." He leaned over and offered her his hand. "It's a pleasure to meet you. I'm Eric Ward."

Madison reached her hand out, surprised by the warmth in his. "Pleasure to meet you, Eric. I can't wait to be your pretend girlfriend tomorrow night."

He grinned at her response. She didn't fail to notice how long he took releasing her hand.

"Tomorrow night you say? I didn't realize it was so soon." He leaned back into the couch and rested his hand along the backside of it. They were too far apart for his arm to be behind her, however, Madison couldn't help thinking how nice it would've felt.

"Yes, tomorrow. The dinner officially starts at seven, but there's a cocktail hour that begins at six. I hope you don't mind going to that. I need all the networking time I can get."

He shook his head. "Nope, I've got a free schedule all day." He cocked an eyebrow at her. "Maybe you should have lunch with me beforehand so we can get to know each other a bit better. I'd hate to do a poor job at playing the supportive boyfriend."

If Madison didn't know any better, it sounded like he just asked her on a date. "Um, sure...that works for me. I don't have much going on tomorrow. I mean, it is Saturday and all, so I have plenty of laundry to do, and I should probably grocery shop and do all the other errands I've put off all week…" She was rambling. Darn nerves. She reached down to scratch an imaginary itch on her knee simply to have something to do with her clammy hands. "What I mean is, yes. Lunch is great."

"Perfect. I know a great sandwich shop that I've been missing this last month."

April, who had been silently observing them the last few minutes, let out a loud yawn at this comment. "Well, I'm glad you made it here safely, Eric. It's been a while since I've seen your beautiful face. I think I'd better go to bed, though." She glanced at the neon-pink sports watch on her wrist then stood. "I'm teaching a five-thirty class in the morning."

"Alright, sis. Thanks for offering up your couch," Eric responded, giving his pillow a dramatic fluff.

April just shook her head and turned toward her room.

Realizing she was about to be left alone with the source of her nerves, Madison jumped up as well. "Uh, yeah, I probably better get to bed, too. Gotta get my...beauty sleep and all that." She didn't wait for his reply. Instead, she followed after April to their rooms.

What Madison secretly wanted to do was go give April a verbal takedown about her misleadings regarding Eric. Considering he sat ten feet away from their doors, though, this wasn't the time.

Instead, she went to her room, letting out a large breath of air as she stepped inside.

What had she gotten herself into?

Chapter 4

By 6 AM, Madison had given up on sleep. She'd been tossing and turning in her bed for the last hour, unable to will her mind back to an unconscious state. There was too much to think about. Too much to worry about, really.

Would the dinner go okay tonight? Would she be socially awkward around him all night like yesterday? Would everyone believe Eric was her boyfriend?

The only thing worse than showing up without a boyfriend would be to show up with a fake boyfriend and everyone find out.

Madison jumped out of bed and began scrambling through her drawers. If there was one thing that made her forget her worries, it was biking.

She found her pair of padded compression leggings and slipped them on. In the beginning, she had rolled her eyes at the other bikers in their neon-colored jerseys and padded biking shorts. She quickly learned that those padded shorts were a necessity, not a fashion statement. A little cushioning went a long way after an hour on a hard, road-bike seat.

Madison slipped on her long-sleeve, nylon jersey as well. She had forgone the neon colors for a more subtle, solid-black number.

After tying her long hair back into a ponytail, she grabbed her clip-on shoes.

Things were still dark as she crept through their apartment. April must've managed to leave the house without waking her brother. Madison hoped to do the same.

When she passed the living room, she heard a faint moan and some movement coming from the couch. She stilled, wondering if Eric could sense her presence. After a second, the movements stopped, and a light snoring sound took its place. She smiled. He snored. That might turn out to be great blackmail material sometime.

Madison managed to sneak out the door without further incident. Grabbing her bike from its locked position on their porch, she walked it out to the main road.

About fifteen minutes later, she was riding free down the street, the wind whipping past her, chilling the tip of her nose.

She needed to think about her strategy at this dinner tonight. She had already left a good impression on Dave. She'd also had pretty good phone interviews with the other managers at the company, a woman named Janet and a man named…Brad? Or was it Brett? She needed to look it up on the company's website.

Connecting with the right people was essential. Despite her confidence in getting the job, she knew good first impressions could be a lifeline. She passed a jogger running at a brisk pace on the sidewalk. The man had dark hair, and her mind immediately went to the dark-haired man sleeping on her couch.

What a surprise he had been. Madison had been expecting a skinny guy wearing glasses and a pocket protector. Instead, he had turned out to be a modern day dreamboat.

She'd spent the entire night failing at getting him out of her mind. She couldn't let that happen tonight. Distraction wasn't an option. He would be nothing more than her arm candy.

Madison ramped up her speed, determination filling her. She definitely wasn't going to waste six years of hard work and schooling on a fleeting pair of blue eyes.

*****

Eric rolled over, the ache in his shoulder reminding him he'd spent the night on a lumpy couch instead of his usual five-star hotel mattress. He groaned and sat up slowly.

The mostly dark room had a faint light filtering through the blinds in front of him. He checked his phone for the time. Seven-thirty. Technically, only five-thirty in California—the time zone he'd been living in the last month.

He flopped back down on his makeshift bed, willing himself to fall back asleep. He knew he wouldn't, though. He was the type that, once he was awake, he stayed awake.

Instead, he let his mind wander back to the last twenty-four hours. Who would've thought he'd be sitting here on his sister's couch? More importantly, who'd have thought he would be playing the pretend boyfriend to her surprisingly attractive roommate?

Not that he had assumed Madison would be ugly. But considering she was scrambling to find a boyfriend, he hadn't expected much.

He'd definitely been wrong.

His first glance at her had momentarily stunned him. And it wasn't that she was trying to be some bombshell dressed to kill. If anything, she'd given off the opposite vibe.

She'd had this rumpled, just-got-out-of-bed look that sent his mind reeling. Her rust colored hair had been tied up loosely with a few stray pieces falling about her face. Her soft-blue eyes were the type that showed every thought in her head. He'd seen as they'd gone from a faint indifference to a sharp disbelief when she'd seen him.

He'd hoped it had been a good disbelief.

Eric had done what he always did in tense situations—reverted to humor. Having his sister there provided plenty of material for teasing and taking the focus off Madison.

It would be interesting to see what today would bring. They had only spent fifteen minutes in each other's presence last night, and most of that time, Madison had been silent.

Reading people wasn't his forte. His skills laid in at understanding algorithms and data structure more than people's feelings. But there'd been some interest coming from Madison, if the constant blush in her cheeks had been any indication.

Lost in his thoughts, he jumped when he heard the front door close. He glanced over his shoulder to see what appeared to be Catwoman walking in the door.

He blinked and squinted his eyes. "April, is that you?" he asked sharply. He wasn't necessarily scared; he just wanted to know exactly what he was dealing with.

Catwoman pulled something from her head that he realized must have been a helmet. She took a few steps forward until the sun, peeking through their windows, finally hit her.

It was Madison—somehow looking even better than she had last night.

She wore some sort of black spandex outfit, one that hugged each of her curves like glue. Her hair had been pulled back in a smooth swoop, and her flushed face spoke of recent exercise.

"No, it's me, Madison." Her voice rang out strong, a contrast to the timid woman she appeared to be last night. She stepped over to the wall and flipped on the light.

"Oh good, I'm glad I didn't have to pull out my self-defense moves." He twisted on the couch so his full body faced her. "What were you doing? Robbing a bank?" He motioned toward her black clothing.

She smirked. "No, I can't add bank robbery to my list of accomplishments yet." She set her helmet and a water bottle down on the counter as she talked. After that, she stood still for a moment, almost as if unsure of what to do.

Eric realized he was taking up most of the common space in the apartment. "Please, come join me on my bed," he said. Then, realizing how that sounded, he added, "I'm just kidding." He stood and quickly grabbed the blankets he'd been sleeping with. "Come have a seat in your living room." There, a nice, safe comment.

She waved her hand at him as he began folding the blankets. "Don't worry about cleaning up; I don't care."

He noted that, despite her statement, she helped him with the folding when she walked in.

"So," he began as he casually sat on one side of the couch. He hoped she'd follow his lead and sit as well. "If you weren't robbing a bank, what were you doing that required you to dress like a ninja at six in the morning?"

Her sing-song laugh rang out in the air. He appreciated the sound. He loved a woman who could laugh easily. Especially at one of his well-timed jokes.

"I'm sorry to say I was just bike riding. Nothing as exciting as you're imagining." She let her hand skim the side of the couch until she finally slid down into the opposite corner. Eric mentally gave himself a fist bump.

"Oh yeah? Road biking or mountain biking?"

"Road biking. I've never gotten into riding trails. Too scary for me. I'm afraid I'll fall and break an arm."

Eric nodded. "I've tried mountain biking a few times, and I have to agree. Most of the time, I'm just hanging onto my handlebars for dear life, praying I don't hit a tree root." Eric drummed his fingers on his knee. "I had a few roommates in college that loved it. Although, I distinctly remember each of them spending a good amount of time in the emergency room."

Madison smiled and begin fiddling with the strands of her ponytail. He watched her fingers as they twirled the auburn hair around and around, mesmerized by the movement.

Obviously, he sat staring too long, because she jumped up, shifting her weight back and forth. "Are you hungry? I'm hungry. I haven't eaten anything yet."

"Sure, I can always eat," he said, a little sad their couch interlude was over.

She turned toward the kitchen. "Let's see what we can come up with."

He studied their apartment a little more as he followed her. It was a nice place, well-kept and neatly decorated. But fairly minimal overall. There wasn't a lot of overly girly or frilly stuff going on.

"What do you feel like?"

Madison had her head stuck in the fridge, and Eric got a great view of her backside. He realized he was gawking and shook his head. Staring down at his socks, he replied, "I don't care...you got any Pop-Tarts?"

"Pop-Tarts?"

The incredulity in her voice made Eric lift his eyes.

"Sorry. Are you Team Toaster Strudels? I mean, I can go either way, but personally—"

"You can't possibly mean you eat *Pop-Tarts* for breakfast?" She leaned on both elbows over the still-open fridge door, her mouth wide open.

He pretended to contemplate her question. "Well, I have been known to eat them for lunch and dinner as well. Generally, I consume them in the morning, though." Eric waited for her response with anticipation. This was the most of her personality she had shown him yet.

"Do you have any idea the ingredients in one of those things? I mean, the nutrition label is any dietician's nightmare!"

"What do you mean? I usually get the strawberry or blueberry ones; that's got to be at least one serving of fruit alone."

If possible, he thought her jaw dropped a little lower. "That's like saying you think an orange Starburst has the same nutritional value as a real orange."

"I prefer the cherry flavor, myself," he replied. "I've heard cherries are high in antioxidants."

"Okay, okay...I have to assume you're joking. Please tell me you're joking." Madison's hand covered her eyes in horror.

Eric grinned. He was having fun messing with her. "I'm pulling your leg, Mads. I know Pop-Tarts and Starbursts are probably shortening my life." He shrugged. "I blame my childhood. Too many cartoon commercials that brainwashed me into thinking they were an acceptable breakfast."

Madison's head went back in the fridge. "That's it, I am making you a healthy—balanced—breakfast." She came up huffing with an armful of eggs, red peppers, and a bag of something green. After setting her load on the counter, she pulled out a frying pan from underneath the stove.

"I thought April said you guys don't provide breakfast?"

She gave him the side eye. A look that was more cute coming from her than intimidating. "We only do in truly desperate circumstances. I'm surprised you're still alive with the diet you probably live on."

He laughed and sat on one of the wooden stools resting on the opposite side of the counter. "I must admit, I'm a little intrigued by you. I don't think I've ever met a girl so worked up about my daily food intake."

Madison stopped chopping the red pepper she'd pulled out and glanced at him. "I can't help it; it's what I do."

"What you do?" Oh no, was she one of those people who felt it was their duty to intervene in other's lives? A self-appointed interventionist?

"Yeah, didn't April tell you? I've spent the last two years getting my Masters in Food Science. Before that, I got my Bachelors in Nutrition."

"Ahhh, it's all making sense now," he said, slapping his hand on the counter. He was surprised at the relief that flooded his mind by her reasonable explanation. Why did he care if his one-night girlfriend was a little psycho or not? "I mean, I know April is kind of a health nut with her exercise classes, so I wasn't sure if it was just her rubbing off on you or something. But clearly, you're just as crazy as she is."

"Hey!" she cried in protest.

Ignoring her response, he leaned in. "So, what healthy and well-balanced breakfast are you making this morning?"

She cocked an eyebrow at him as she scraped the red peppers into the hot skillet. They immediately began to sizzle and pop. "I'm not sure if you deserve this anymore, but I am making an omelette."

"Hmm, well, so far it smells delicious." Watching her work was fascinating. She was so focused that he could study her without her seeing. Just as he'd noticed last night, she was a natural beauty. Her pulled-up hair only enhanced the fine bone structure of her face. Despite her delicate features, she had a full mouth that currently puckered in a pout. She probably had no idea she made that face when she concentrated.

Suddenly, an image flashed through his mind about what it'd be like to kiss those full lips. The thought both surprised him and made him leery. He had to be careful. There was no way he would get involved with his little sister's roommate. That was a can of worms nobody needed to open.

"You're not allergic to anything, are you?"

Madison's question brought him back to the present.

"Um, nope. Not that I know of."

She nodded and went back to her work. He saw she had managed to chop some onions and spinach during his musings. She reached for the eggs now.

Eric watched her hands, their sure movements suddenly hesitant. Madison tapped an egg lightly on the edge of the pan, the force clearly not enough because the egg remained in its whole state. She paused before trying again, this time with more impact. She was rewarded with a splattering of egg yolk and shells.

"Ah, darn it," she cried out. She quickly reached for a towel and began mopping up her mess.

"Not a fan of cracking eggs?" he asked, slowly pushing himself up from the stool.

Madison's face scrunched. "I've never quite mastered the art of it." She shrugged her shoulders as she tossed the dirty towel into the sink. "I went to school to learn about *what* to cook, not necessarily *how* to cook it."

Eric had walked around to the other side of the counter. He reached across her, grabbing two eggs from the carton. If he didn't know better, he would've sworn she had held her breath during the split second he was near her.

"I don't want to brag, but I'm something of an expert when it comes to cracking eggs." Having said this, he deftly took an egg in each hand and rapped them both on the side of the counter at the same time. In perfect unison, the shells cracked, and he dumped the clear egg whites and perfectly whole yolks into the hot pan.

"What the...how did you do that?" Madison cried. She shoved her hands on her hips. "I thought you said you ate Pop-Tarts for breakfast every day."

Eric grinned. "I may have had a small stint as a line order cook in college. There was a local coffee place that specialized in breakfast sandwiches. Guess who became the shop's top egg scrambler between their sophomore and senior years?" He pointed his thumb at himself. "This guy."

"Okay, you're on egg duty," she said, sliding the carton over to him. "We'll need four more, I think."

Eric made quick work of the rest. Finished, he grabbed the half-empty cardboard container and moved to put it back in the fridge.

Madison stepped forward and began scrambling in the various vegetables.

He found his way back to the stool behind the counter. Tapping his fingers, he asked, "So, now that I know you're a nutritionist, tell me a little bit more about the job you're applying for."

Her hands slowed their stirring, but she never took her eyes from her work. "It's a position with one of the biggest vitamin and supplement manufacturers in the world. Have you ever heard of Sube Nutritionals?"

Eric nodded his head. "I have. I'm pretty sure my mom forced me to take vitamins made by them when I was a kid."

Madison smiled, finally lifting those pretty blue eyes to meet his. "She probably did, and you should thank her for that." Walking over to the cabinet, she grabbed some plates. "The position is for a food scientist, which basically entails taking care of all the formulas and recipes for their products."

"Like making sure a vitamin C actually has vitamin C in it?"

"Yeah, although, it's a little more complicated than that. It includes working with ingredient suppliers, testing for food safety, estimating the shelf-life of products, the scalability..."

Her voice trailed off, and Eric assumed she'd look overwhelmed at all that would be expected of her. But instead, what he saw was excitement. Her eyes gleamed as if she couldn't wait to take up all the challenges.

"Well, it sounds like quite the job. I'll do my best to make sure I don't screw things up for you tonight." He added a wink.

Madison laughed as she set her load down, the ceramic plates making a slight clatter against the countertop. "Well, I'm actually feeling pretty confident about the position. I don't think there's too much you could do to ruin it for me unless you don't show up." Her face fell slightly at her last words.

Eric instinctively reached out and covered one of her hands with his. "Don't worry, I keep my promises. I'll be there."

He surprised himself with the gesture, but he seemed to shock Madison more. Her face flushed a bright red, and she immediately began scooping eggs onto the plates.

"Yes, well, I won't hold you to anything besides this night," Madison said, holding a plate out to him. "I know you have a life of your own."

Her comment seemed to hold some sort of weight to it. Almost as if she wanted to remind him that no real relationship would come out of this. It was purely business.

"Thank you," he simply said as he took the plate. He couldn't help wondering about the comment. Was she trying to hint that her feelings were otherwise engaged? That wouldn't make sense. She would've just taken whoever that guy was to the dinner tonight. Whatever her reasons, she clearly didn't want anything to come of this weekend. Which was fine with Eric. He didn't live the kind of life that supported committed relationships. He was hardly in one spot long enough to form one, let alone keep it up.

"Oh, I forgot forks." Madison turned and opened a drawer behind her, the sound of utensils rattling as she yanked it open.

As soon as he had a fork in his hand, Eric dug in. "Wow, this is delicious. I know you said cooking isn't your thing, but you're actually pretty good."

She tried to bite back a smile. "Thank you. I wouldn't say eggs are the trickiest dish, but I'm glad you like it."

They ate in silence until they were interrupted by the front door swinging open.

April walked in wearing a pair of headphones and jamming to a song. When she saw Madison and Eric, she stopped. "Well, look at you two. Up and at 'em on a Saturday morning."

"I have to say, this isn't normal for me. But with service like this"—Eric motioned toward his almost empty plate—"I could probably get up early every day."

His sister eyed the counter. "Wow, you must have been super nice to Madison for her to have made you breakfast." She wiggled her eyebrows at Madison.

He wondered what that meant. Girls and their silent communication with each other. It was like a secret language.

Madison cleared her throat loudly and pursed her lips. More secret language.

"I only made this because your brother informed me that Pop-Tarts are his regular breakfast. *Pop-Tarts*." She shook her head. "You might as well sign yourself up for an early funeral right now."

"Ha ha, I'd like to say I'm surprised, but I'm not." April had pulled the earbuds out and placed them and her phone on the counter. "I'm pretty sure he started those habits back in high school."

"Yeah, you used to be a lot more fun back then—before you turned into Ms. Health and Fitness." Eric turned back to his plate and took another bite. "I'm pretty sure you polished off a fair number of Pop-Tarts back in the day yourself."

"Did you save any for me?" April asked, ignoring his comment. She grabbed a glass out of the cupboard and filled it with water.

Madison motioned toward the stove. "Yeah, it's staying warm in the pan. Can you grab me a glass of water?"

"Mmph. Me too." The food in Eric's mouth muffled his request.

"The things I do for you people," April mumbled, grabbing two more glasses.

"How were your classes?" Madison asked.

"Pretty good. My 5:30 class was normal. My 6:30 class was huge, though. The other instructor called in sick, so I got all her students." April shook her head. "We were packed in like sardines." She looked over at Madison and scanned her outfit. "Did you go on a bike ride this morning?"

"Yeah, it's been a while, so I'll probably be sore tomorrow." Madison took her plate over to the sink. "But it was a good ride."

"I plan to do some water aerobics in a couple hours myself," Eric added, puffing his chest out. "I can't go too long in between workouts or I start losing muscle mass." He flexed one of his arms, causing Madison to snort and April to groan.

"You are ridiculous," his sister told him as she began eating.

He just grinned as he followed Madison over to the sink. "So," he said, his focus now on her, "are we still good for lunch today?"

Madison seemed pinned to the sink for a moment, unable to move. Eric wondered if his nearness had anything to do with her tension.

"Uh, yeah," she finally said, relaxing ever so slightly. "Yeah, lunch still works. What time?"

"Hmm…" He purposely leaned over her to put his plate in the open dishwasher. She rewarded the move with another statuesque pose. Alright. He needed to stop teasing her. "Let's just go with noon? I have to check on my storage unit and run a few errands this morning. I'll probably be back a little after 11:30 and we can leave then?"

Madison had managed to inch herself away from him, her flushed face studying the ground. "Yep, sounds great. I'm going to go shower, but I'll see you then."

With that, she scampered out of the kitchen and down the hallway.

April, who had been watching their interaction, narrowed her eyes at him. "What exactly do you think you're doing to my roommate?"

Chapter 5

An hour later, Madison came out of her room, freshly showered and changed. She'd actually been ready for a while, but she wanted to make sure Eric had left to run his errands before she came out. A bit immature? Possibly. But there was something about him that made her so jittery. He hadn't done anything overly forward or brash, but she couldn't help turning into a pool of nerves around him.

She walked into the living area, glad to see April sitting on the couch with her laptop open in front of her.

"Why did you lie to me?" she asked, compulsively reaching over to straighten the books that had tilted slightly on their bookshelf.

Her abrupt question made April's eyebrows lift. "Lie to you? About what?"

"About your brother."

The surprise in April's eyes softened slightly. "What do you mean? I didn't lie to you about anything."

"You led me to believe that he was some nerdy computer geek with no social skills." Satisfied their reading material was properly situated, she flopped onto the couch, catching a faint woodsy smell as she did. She inhaled once more, realizing mid-breath that it must have been a residual scent from Eric sleeping there last night.

"Well, I wouldn't rate his social skills as top notch—" April continued.

"April! Your brother is a total hottie," she responded, coming back to the conversation. "Why the heck didn't you tell me? And how in the world is he still single and floating around like you say?" She willed herself to stop sniffing the air like a bloodhound. Eric's scent meant nothing to her.

Her roommate closed her laptop slowly. "Okay, my brother may be slightly better looking than I led you to believe." She scrunched up her face. "Although, if you'd been teased by him your entire life, you'd probably have a hard time seeing him as anything remotely attractive, too."

Madison folded her arms stiffly.

"Anyway, yes, he is moderately good looking," April hurried to continue, "but everything else I told you is true. He *is* a total computer geek. And he does lack any normal social interaction. His job is his life. He freelances, which basically means companies work him like a dog until he moves on to his next project. I don't think he's stayed in the same place longer than two months in the last four years."

Madison chewed her lip as she listened. "He seems to be doing fine to me. If anyone has been socially awkward, it's been me."

April stifled a smile. "I noticed that. You have seemed a little infatuated with him."

Madison could feel her cheeks warming—not that she cared about April's assumptions. But if she noticed something, Eric probably had too. "It's just because he's not what I expected," she finally said, throwing her hands up. "I was expecting a skinny guy with four eyes. Not some dreamy computer technician."

"Haha, don't worry, Madison. Like you said, this is just a one night thing." April lifted her brow, making her words seem more of a question than a statement.

"Yes...of course."

April turned back to her computer, waving her hand dismissively. "By next week, he'll be gone and out of your hair."

Madison wasn't sure whether that made her feel better or worse.

*****

"So, we are in a committed relationship. Have you set up any parameters about how long we've been dating?" Eric glanced at Madison as he unwrapped his food.

They were eating at the sandwich shop he had mentioned. Madison had to give it to him, the place was a hidden gem. The menu had a bizarre fusion of cuisines. Everything from curry-seasoned deli meats to Korean-BBQ-flavored cheesesteaks. Madison had gone with a somewhat safe choice of a goat cheese turkey sandwich.

"No, I didn't give any details. We're starting with a blank palette." She glanced at him, wishing she could mirror the relaxed vibe he put off, leaning back in his fitted t-shirt and Denver Broncos baseball hat. "So, what do you want for our relationship?"

Eric shrugged. "Whatever is easiest to remember is good with me. Let's say we have been dating for about a year—that seems pretty standard."

She tried to focus on her food and not the adorable way he smiled when he teased. "That works. So we've been dating a year. How did we meet? Through a mutual friend?"

He nodded. "My buddy gave me your number. It took me a few months to get up the guts to call you, because we all know you're way out of my league..."

Madison unconsciously uncrossed and recrossed her legs, looking anywhere but at him.

"...but I finally did, and you said yes."

She cleared her throat. "Alright, so we went on our first date. It was dinner and a movie—"

"Because I'm clearly the most boring, unimaginative guy out there," Eric cut in dryly.

"Okay,"—she cocked an eyebrow—"what do you want our first date to be?" Madison preferred his clear banter as opposed to the sly compliments he kept sliding in. When they had left the house earlier, the first thing he'd told her was how beautiful she looked. Something that both pleased her and put her on edge.

"Hmm, let me think. Do you like arcades?"

"Like a video game arcade?"

He nodded and took another bite.

"I can't remember the last time I've been to one. Probably back in elementary school."

"You haven't been to an arcade since elementary school?" Eric almost dropped his sandwich.

She tried not to smile at his ridiculousness. "No. Is that unusual? Do most twenty-something females you know frequently visit arcades?"

"No, but they *should.* Alright, our first date was at an arcade where you rekindled your love with video game classics."

"Like Skee-Ball?"

He rubbed his eyelids, grimacing. "I don't even know how to respond to that. Skee-Ball? I'm talking Pac-Man, Asteroids, Street Fighter... None of those ringing a bell?"

Madison had to fight back a laugh now. She grabbed her cup and sipped lemon water through the straw. "Nope."

"Alright, at some point in the next week, I am going to take you to an arcade, and you are getting a crash course in Video Games 101." He lifted his cup for emphasis, the brown liquid inside sloshing around the clear cup.

She laughed. "Alright, so our first date was a unique and memorable night at an arcade. Let's say we followed that up with some ice cream."

"Sounds good. What other information do we need to know about each other?" Eric took a swig of his soda.

"I don't know. Maybe I should know more about your job. I know you do something with computers? And I know you travel a ton." She was proud of herself. They'd had a solid ten minutes of conversation, and she was pretty sure she hadn't blushed once.

"You could say I'm never *not* traveling. But yeah, I do freelance computer programming. Generally, companies call me when they want a rehaul of the software programs they are using. I work on their data integration and strategies, front-end development, back-end development, site deployment...pretty exciting stuff."

Madison stared at him for a second, the technical terms turning her mind numb. "Yeah...I'm probably just going to say you do computer programming."

He lifted one of his french fries in a mock toast.

"Do you have any idea how bad those are for your heart?" she asked after looking pointedly at the fry.

He took another handful of fries and dramatically dunked them into his ketchup before shoving them in his mouth. "Do *you* have any idea how delicious these are?" He nodded toward the salad on her plate. "You can't tell me you're really enjoying that thing."

Madison looked down at the lackluster side salad he referred to. Using her fork, she pushed aside one of the limp spinach leaves, hating that he was right.

"That's another aspect we could play up," he continued. "Your constant attempt to turn me to the dark side of eating healthy, and my firm resolve to stay strong with my fried foods and sugary drinks." He shook his cup for emphasis.

"That is probably one of the most realistic components of our relationship yet," Madison responded before biting her tongue. Why did she say that? They weren't in a relationship.

Eric didn't seem to notice. "You're probably right. So, I know you like bike riding in a Catwoman outfit at extremely early hours. What else should I know about you?"

Madison had to use all her self-control to not spit out the water she had just sipped. "You are ridiculous," she finally said through her laughter. "It was not a Catwoman outfit! It was just black leggings and a black long-sleeve shirt." She couldn't remember the last time she had laughed so much with someone.

"Alright, so anything besides bike riding?"

"I actually like cooking. I'm no expert, but I love seeing how ingredients can be combined. I guess I like reading when I have the time." She shrugged. "I'm not too interesting."

"What? Don't sell yourself short; you've got a lot more going for you than most girls."

Madison desperately wanted to ask what exactly it was she had going for her, but Eric had moved on.

"I don't know if we have any hobbies that really align." He crumpled his wrapper into a ball, tossing it lightly onto his tray. "I like hiking, occasionally. Obviously, I'm into all sorts of geeky technical stuff."

"Your sister mentioned you like chess."

His eyes lit up at her comment. "I do. Do you play?"

For some reason, Madison had a hard time imagining the man in front of her sitting down for an intellectual game of chess. He was much too attractive for such a nerdy pursuit. "Occasionally. I wouldn't say I'm very good, though. My dad really loves it and tried to teach me the game growing up." She lifted her palms. "I never took to it as well as my brothers did, but I can tell my kings from my rooks."

Eric snapped his fingers. "Add that to the list of things we need to do this week. Play a game of chess."

Madison mentally added up all the things they had "scheduled" to do. They would be spending a lot more time together than she had planned.

Both of them had finished their food by then, and the conversation wound down.

Eric looked at her tray. "You done?"

She nodded. "Yes, thank you again. This place is really good. I'll have to remember it." Automatically, she stacked their wrappers and plates into a pile. Pulling a handful of napkins out of the plastic dispenser, she then began wiping down their relatively clean table.

"Yeah, I don't think too many people know about it, but I always pay them a visit when I'm in town." Eric's gaze sobered a little as he stood. "I guess it's one of the few traditions I have in my life."

Madison paused her cleaning, curious about the emotion she saw on his face. "April said you got rid of the apartment you were leasing. So, you technically have no place to call home?"

He grabbed the stack of trash she'd made. "Nope, no homebase. I mean, I have a storage unit where I keep all my stuff, but I'm around so infrequently it was pointless to continue paying rent."

Madison wanted to question him more on the topic, but when she opened her mouth, he cut her off.

"You ready to go?" he asked as he deposited their trash.

Madison set aside her curiosities and her now dirty napkins. They were, apparently, going to have plenty of time together the rest of the week to talk, why push it?

Chapter 6

Madison knew she needed to look the part tonight. The dinner was a formal event, not quite black tie, but a cocktail dress would be appropriate—at least, according to Dave's receptionist.

She hadn't gotten much detail about the humanitarian project the company sponsored. After a quick Google search, she discovered it had something to do with providing supplements to malnutritioned kids. Considering their industry, it seemed appropriate.

Standing in front of her closet, she examined her choices. She didn't attend a lot of formal events, so she basically had two options.

The first was a knee-length cream dress that she'd worn to a friend's wedding last summer. It had a high neckline, offset by a loose, A-line silhouette.

The second option was a little more dramatic. The top was intricately beaded and dipped into a low V neckline. The bottom half of the dress had a smooth, silky fabric that flowed effortlessly over her legs with a slit riding up to her knee. The midnight-blue fabric blended perfectly with the glistening black beading on top. She'd bought the sultry dress for a Christmas party earlier this year but hadn't been able to attend. It still had the tags on it.

Madison took both options out and hung them on her doorframe, eyeing them from a distance.

The safe choice would be the cream dress. It would fit in with almost any environment. But she knew she looked better in the blue one. Her mind flashed to Eric. She tried to ignore the fact that he tipped the scales. For some reason, she wanted to turn his head tonight.

Even as the thought passed through her mind, she felt like rolling her eyes. How ridiculous could she get? Eric had no interest in her. He was doing this purely as a favor. She needed to make sure his meaningless flirting didn't stir up any lasting emotions in her.

Despite her resolve, she grabbed the blue dress and hung it on the doorframe. It was the logical choice, really. The navy color was more slimming.

With a sigh, she strutted into the bathroom, determined to put Eric from her mind. She had more important things to worry about tonight, anyway. Like the job offer on the line. The whole reason she was even in this mess.

She pulled out her curling iron and plugged it in. She began sectioning off her reddish-brown hair with a large clip.

First priority for the evening would be getting face time with Dave again. His support would be crucial. It would also be good to chat with some of the other people she'd had preliminary interviews with.

Madison sprayed her locks with a texturizer and began curling the ends, making sure to avoid burning her fingertips. Tonight would go great. She was good at events like this. Mingling and making small talk came naturally for her, so there shouldn't be any concerns.

Her mind trailed back to the pair of blue eyes and sly grin she couldn't get out of her head.

Hopefully, there wouldn't be any concerns.

*****

Eric finished adjusting his cufflinks as he heard Madison's door opening. Sure, cufflinks were probably a little pompous, but he wanted to show Madison that he wasn't some sloppy tech geek.

He knew what most preconceived notions about computer guys were.

Most people assumed he would be the type that worked insanely late hours, lived on fast food, and thought graphic T-shirt's were suitable for every occasion.

Realistically, maybe about half of that was true. He did work insanely late hours and did eat fast food too often, but he could clean up decently if he tried.

Eric adjusted his suit jacket as he saw Madison come around the corner. The second she came into view, though, he froze.

He thought he'd seen Madison at all her extremes. He'd seen casual Madison in her jeans the first night; he'd seen her sweaty, post-workout look this morning; and he thought he'd seen her all dolled up at lunch this afternoon. But clearly, lunch had just been a warm-up drill, because she quite literally took his breath away.

Her dark-blue dress seemed glued to her body. It shifted and slinked with every step she took. She had done something different to her hair, as well. Was it always wavy like that? It looked all soft and flowy around her face. While she had been beautiful before, she mesmerized him now.

"You...I..." He cleared his throat and tried to get something coherent out. "You look amazing. I'm not sure if I'm up to your standards."

The familiar blush he'd seen countless times now made its appearance. Madison was one of those people with flawless, fair skin. But it was also the kind of skin that displayed every hint of emotion inside her.

She ducked her head slightly and fumbled with the bag in her hand. "Thank you. You look great, too." As she eyed him from head to toe, Eric felt a similar warmth in his own face. "Where did you get that suit? There's no way that was packed in your luggage." She looked pointedly at the small suitcase Eric had gotten used to traveling with.

"I'm like Mary Poppins. You never know what I'm going to pull out of my bag." He gave her a wink. "But this may have also been one of the reasons I needed to stop by my storage unit today."

She nodded, shifting her weight from one heeled shoe to the other. How women walked in shoes like that was a mystery to him, but they sure did look good on her.

Knowing he needed to stop gawking, he came around from his side of the couch and offered her his arm.

Adopting his best British accent, he asked, "Shall we go, my lady?"

A grin hinted at Madison's mouth as she tucked her hand into his arm.

Before they reached the door, though, he stopped. "Someone should get our picture. It's not every day I look this good." He actually wasn't much of a picture guy. The number of pictures he had from the last few years of life was probably less than most people took in a month. But it seemed like a moment they should capture.

"Well, April's teaching a class tonight, so I think a self timer is our only option," she responded, biting her lip.

"Self timer it is." He pulled out his phone and glanced around the room, looking for a prop. The kitchen countertop seemed the best option; it was the highest flat spot in the room. "Could you be my model?" he asked, nodding toward the entryway. "Stand over by the wall, and I'll angle this on you."

Madison did as he directed, although, she dragged her feet all the way there. "Do we really need a picture of this?" she asked as he fiddled with the timer options.

He raised his eyebrows, trying his best to look hurt. "This might be one of our last dates before you break up with me. I'm going to need something to remember you by when I'm wetting my pillow with tears every night."

Madison didn't even try to hold back her smile this time, and those full lips were doing all sorts of things with his heart. "You're ridiculous," she said.

Trying to keep his mind on his task, he turned back to the counter. With the help of some decorative candles smelling strongly of vanilla and cinnamon, he propped his phone up at the right angle. He glanced at the screen, double-checking that every inch of Madison was in it—maybe even triple-checking if just to get a moment to stare at her again. "Alright, I think it's good." He looked up. "Are you ready? We'll have to the count of ten."

She nodded, and he quickly tapped the screen before running over.

He quietly counted down as he moved. "Ten, nine..."

By the time he got to number six, he'd reached Madison. Wrapping an arm lightly around her waist, he couldn't help noticing how stiffly she held her body. Tilting his head close, he whispered, "Smile!" before the lens shuttered for the picture.

Eric had planned on immediately letting her go, but something rooted him to the spot. He wasn't sure if it was the warmth of her body under his hand, or maybe it was the heady, flowery scent that seemed to surround her. Whatever it was, Eric found his eyes locked on hers, their crystal blue boring into him.

The overwhelming desire to kiss her raced through his mind. He slid his arm further around her narrow waist, drawing her closer to him, until they were inches apart. The stiffness in her body was gone, and she had almost eased into his side now. A small part of his brain screamed at him to stop. This was his little sister's roommate. This wasn't someone he could get involved with before taking off again.

But that part of his brain clearly had little say in the matter as he focused on how good she felt in his arms. Madison obviously wasn't thinking, either, as she lifted one hand to rest on his chest. Unless he imagined it, she had tilted her face toward his, her wide eyes relaxing as they closed the gap—

Crack!

The loud noise snapped them apart. Eric felt like he'd been doused with cold water. What was he thinking?

He looked over at the source of the sound. The candle he had been balancing his phone against had slipped. The phone had toppled to the ground and landed with a loud thud on the wood floor.

Bending over, Eric picked up the small device, checking for cracks or scratches. He tried to appear calm even though his heart was beating a million miles an hour. "Well, guess I got my money's worth out of this phone case," he said. His voice sounded strangely hoarse, as if it hadn't been used in days.

Madison tittered nervously. "I guess so." She began twirling one strand of her hair, a tick he'd noticed as a sure sign of her nerves.

Thinking quickly, Eric reached forward and pulled her into a close embrace again. He had gotten them into this mess, so he would get them out of it. "Alright, one quick selfie in case that first one didn't turn out." He held his phone out in front of them and yelled, "Cheeeese!" before snapping a photo. As he showed the picture to Madison, her nervous giggles melted into that beautiful sing-song laugh he loved.

"You look absurd in this," she said, holding the phone out to him again.

"Me? I feel like I'm pulling a pretty suave look there." He smiled as he slid the phone back into his pocket. Hopefully, they'd be able to move on with the night despite that awkward interlude. "Alright, enough shenanigans. We better get going or else Cinderella's going to be late to the ball."

"Yes. Then what would Prince Charming do?" was all she said as they headed out the door.

*****

Madison slid into the passenger seat of Eric's rental car, grateful to have at least ten seconds of solitude before he got in next to her. She needed to gain control of the situation. No more of these mind games Eric was apparently so fond of.

She'd been a split second from kissing him just then. Something she had no intention of repeating. This was business only. She couldn't let emotions get involved. Because, as cute as he was, she could tell he was flighty. If Madison got involved with someone, it would be a committed relationship. She wasn't the kiss-and-run type. And she didn't want her heart to get broken by a guy who was.

As Eric started the engine, she fingered the black drop earrings she had in her ears. They played off the black beading in her dress perfectly.

"So..." Eric said, letting the car idle in the parking spot.

Please don't bring up that almost kiss, Madison thought weakly to herself. She hoped to just pretend it had never happened. When he turned to her with lifted eyebrows, she started formulating an explanation why it meant nothing.

Luckily, he continued before she spoke. "...are you going to give me the address to this place, or am I just going to have to guess?"

She hoped her relief wasn't visibly evident. "Oh! I'm sorry. I totally forgot." She scrambled through her purse, looking for her phone. When she finally had it, she referenced the email with the instructions for the evening. "Here, let me just put this in my GPS." A few seconds later, a monotone woman's voice filled the car. "Starting route to 5382 State Street..."

Eric put the car in reverse. "And here we go."

The place was relatively close to Madison's apartment. Within twenty minutes, they were pulling up to the large reception hall, the type people rented for high-end weddings or events.

Eric whistled at the "Valet Parking Only" sign. "Man, your company is legit. I'm just happy when one of my employers gives me a Starbucks gift card or something."

She had to agree with him. Pulling her nose from the window, she said, "Well, I'm not an employee yet, so don't get lax tonight, or I might not get the job."

"You're right," he said as he smoothly turned the car into the lot, "and you haven't even been to one of their holiday parties yet. I bet they make this one look shabby."

Madison just laughed as they pulled up to the curb. A guy in his early twenties briskly opened her door and welcomed her.

She turned and set her heels on the concrete, her dress gliding smoothly across the leather seat before she stood.

Eric came around to her side, and Madison once more admired how sleek he looked in his dark suit. The cut was perfect; it had obviously been tailored to him. She wondered once again about his career. From all appearances, he seemed like he must have been successful. But then, why did he choose to live such a transient life? There had to be more settled opportunities for someone with his skills.

He pulled her from her thoughts by grabbing her hand. "You ready?" he asked with raised eyebrows.

This wasn't the night to muse about her pretend boyfriend. "Yes. Let's go." She stepped forward with a sure step, ignoring the butterflies shooting through her stomach for more reasons than one.

They walked into the entrance, the high ceilings and wide hall creating a dramatic scene.

Madison was so busy taking it all in she didn't even hear the hostess welcome them and ask what party they were here for. Luckily, Eric took charge.

"We're here for the Sube Nutritionals dinner."

"Perfect." The woman smiled sweetly at them. "Right down this hall. You're in the main banquet room tonight."

"Thank you." His firm grasp on her hand directed them to the end of the hall where there was a set of tall double doors. A line of two or three people were checking in with a woman holding a tablet.

When they reached her, she quickly asked, "Can I get your names?"

"Yes, it should be under Madison Hudson and Ethan..." She stalled, suddenly not able to recall what she'd chosen as her fake boyfriend's last name.

"Ward. Ethan Ward," Eric said from her side.

The woman's smile warmed when she glanced at Eric, and Madison felt a jealous set of claws coming out.

"Thank you," she said, juvenilely reaching out for the set of auction numbers the woman offered Eric. Without a backwards glance, Madison pulled on his arm, directing him toward the doors and away from the woman's open gaze.

Her discomfort was appeased, though, when he readily followed her. "So, looks like there's going to be some sort of auction?" He indicated to the numbers in her hand.

She looked down. "Yeah, it must be for the charity." Each paddle she held had an oversized number twenty-four printed on them.

He found her hand again and squeezed it as they walked into the room. "You ready for this?"

"Let's hope so."

The place buzzed with people and conversations. Madison felt a little overwhelmed at the enormity of the group until she remembered that this was a charity dinner. There was likely a bunch of donors here in addition to Sube Nutritional employees.

She scanned the room, hoping to see a familiar face. She was finally rewarded when she saw Janet, one of the managers she'd met in the first round of interviews. She nodded in the woman's direction, and Eric silently followed her.

"Janet," Madison said, putting a burst of enthusiasm in her voice, as they approached. "It's so good to see you again."

Janet turned slightly, her face lighting up in recognition after a second. "Madison, right?"

Madison was just grateful Janet remembered her name. Nothing was worse than one of those awkward conversations where one person had no idea who they were speaking with. "Yes, I interviewed with you about a week ago."

"Of course, I remember. I'm assuming Dave invited you here tonight?"

"Yes," Madison replied, her eyebrows raised. If she was lucky, Janet would be able to give her some insider information.

Janet obviously noticed her questioning glance. "Dave said he invited all the final candidates tonight. He thought it'd be a good opportunity for you to get a feel for the company."

Other candidates? As much as Madison had tried not to, she had almost convinced herself the job was hers. But if Dave still had others on his list, things were still on the line.

"Hi, my name is Janet. I'm one of the managing lab techs here."

Madison pulled herself out of her musings to see Janet and Eric shaking hands. "Oh, I'm sorry, this is my boyfriend, Eri—Ethan." Whew, she would need to work on that.

"Pleasure to meet you, Janet. From all Madison's told me about the job, this sounds like a wonderful company." Eric's manners were perfection.

Janet gave him a bright smile. Good thing she had to be somewhere in her late forties, or Madison's jealousy might have crept out again.

"Oh, how wonderful to have you here tonight. It's great to get a glimpse of people's personal lives."

"Yeah," Eric continued, "nothing like seeing someone's other half." He draped his arm around Madison and pulled her in tight.

Madison was beginning to think he was a whole lot better at this acting stuff than her.

"My other half is around here somewhere, too," Janet said, scanning the room. "He said he was going to get something to drink, but I haven't seen him since. He's probably hiding out in the foyer, watching a football game."

Madison smiled and asked a few more questions about Janet's family. She had two kids, both early teenagers and a handful of trouble, according to her. After a minute, one of Janet's colleagues waved her over to another group, and they parted ways.

Madison scanned the room for another target to schmooze with.

A tall woman in a black dress caught her eye. She leaned in and tapped Eric's arm, catching another whiff of his woodsy cologne. It was a scent she could get used to. "I see the other woman I interviewed with; her name is Rachel. Let's go talk to her."

Eric obediently followed, obviously willing to play his role for the night.

A similar conversation ensued. They chatted about their interview, and Madison introduced Eric to her as her boyfriend named Ethan. Madison decided to see if Rachel had any additional insights about the job.

"So, do you know if Dave invited anyone else interviewing for the position tonight?" She tried to make the comment seem casual.

Rachel scrunched her nose in thought. "I wouldn't be surprised. He likes people to meet the whole team before making hiring decisions." She eyed Madison, almost as if contemplating her next comment. "Don't worry, you did a great job in your interview, and you're definitely qualified for the position." She glanced between Eric and Madison and smiled. "Don't let nerves ruin a fun night out for you two!"

"Oh, I'm not worried," Madison said, her voice much too high-pitched and cheery. "I was just curious if I would meet the others here."

Eric put his arm around her once again, like a protective cocoon. Her skin tingled from the heat of it, and she tried to keep her mind on the conversation.

"I keep telling her not to stress; there's no one else as good at what she does than Mads here."

He pulled her in close and kissed the top of her head, amplifying the skin tingling into a downright shiver.

Not that the kiss had been anything dramatic. Heavens, her grandpa could have gotten away with a similar gesture. But when Eric did it, it felt more suggestive. Maybe it was the way his suit brushed against her bare skin, or the strength of his arm holding her exactly where he wanted to. Whatever it was, it got to her.

Rachel seemed convinced as well. "Well, I hope you cuties have a fun night. And my fingers are crossed for you for the position." With that, she was off, talking to other people, and Eric and Madison were alone.

Madison knew she should have been looking for others to chat with, but she needed a moment to think. First off, she had to remind herself that she and Eric were not really an item, despite how comfortable she was beginning to feel next to him. She took a step back so his arm no longer wrapped around her. Second off, the job wasn't as guaranteed as she had assumed. Rachel and Janet seemed to like her, but the key decision-maker had to be Dave. He would be the one she needed to really impress this evening.

"How am I doing, snookums?" Eric whispered in her ear.

His warm breath surprised her, and all her thoughts about the job vanished. "You're doing great, *Ethan*," she said, turning her head to face him. She'd actually noticed he'd used the short version of her name, Mads, several times since they had met. Normally, she wasn't a huge fan of the nickname, but the way it rolled off his tongue was somehow acceptable.

He straightened with a smile. "You know, I've always wondered what it would be like to have another name." He tapped his temple as if thinking. "Ethan doesn't sound so bad, does it?"

"Ha ha, I think just about any name would sound good on you," she said before she could stop herself. She immediately tried to cover her comment. "Are you thirsty? I'm thirsty. Where's the bar area? It's probably around here. We should get something to drink." She followed up her rapidfire comments by spinning on her heel and heading toward the bar in the corner.

She didn't wait to see Eric's reaction, but she wouldn't have been surprised to find him laughing at her. She was such a doof.

"What can I get you two tonight?" the bartender asked as they approached.

"I'll just have a water," Madison said, playing with the stack of napkins on the counter.

Eric glanced at her, then at the bartender. "I'll have one, too."

Two minutes later, they were walking away with glasses of ice water in hand and nowhere to go.

"So, is there anyone else you want to talk to specifically?" Eric asked after they stood for a minute in silence.

Madison gripped her dewy glass with both hands, glancing around. "I probably should. It would help to know more people."

"What about the boss? The guy that you interviewed with? Is he here yet?"

"Dave? No, I haven't seen him. He's ultimately the one I need to impress." She ran a finger around the edge of her cup, debating whether to tell him how she'd expected to be the only job candidate here tonight. "I didn't realize he invited some of the other interviewers. I kind of thought I was the only one he asked to come. I obviously jumped the gun a little." How naive she had been. This was the real world; nothing was guaranteed.

"Madison, you need to get out of your head." He eyed her for a second before sighing and setting his glass of water on a nearby table. "Alright, I only give my pump-up talks to really special people, but you're clearly in need tonight."

She narrowed her eyes as he braced his hands on both of her shoulders, giving them a light squeeze.

In a quiet but serious tone, he said, "Madison, you are not just some other job candidate out here tonight. You are

Madison Penelope Hudson the First. You have a Bachelors and a Masters degree in eating vegetables—"

"Nutrition and Food Science," she cut in.

"—you graduated top of your class." He ignored her as his voice slowly escalated in power. "Top honors. Phi Beta Kappa Sailormoon Lightning Bolt—"

"That's not a real thing—"

"—you nailed your interview with one of the top vitamin companies in the world. The *leader* in chewable vitamin C and fruity flavored multivitamins."

The hilarity of the moment enveloped Madison.

"And now, you are at their charity dinner with one of the hottest guys you've ever met at your beck and call. The second Dave walks into this room, he's going to know you're the right choice. You are Madison Hudson!"

His voice finished in a stage whisper, and Madison could barely hold back her laugh. When it was clear he was done, she began a quiet round of applause to which he responded with a bow.

"Have you ever considered a career transition to motivational speaking?" she asked when he straightened.

Eric wiggled his eyebrows. "No," he said, "but I should, shouldn't I?"

She took a sip of her water, but not before she gave him a playful shove. "And for the record, my middle name is Kay, not Penelope."

"Huh, I thought Madison Penelope had a nice ring to it," he said.

She rolled her eyes when a movement by the door caught her attention. She saw Dave walking in with a woman that must have been his wife on his arm. It was go-time.

She set her cup of water next to Eric's. "There, you see the man walking in?" she asked.

Eric nodded.

"That's Dave. The CEO. He's the one we have to make a good impression on tonight."

Eric linked his fingers together and reached out his arms, pretending to crack his knuckles. "Let's do this."

*****

It was interesting, seeing Madison from this perspective. The vibe she'd given off at lunch had been a very confident, sure-of-herself woman. Tonight, he'd seen another side of her. Her vulnerable side.

Being the one she leaned on in those moments of doubt had been nice. He hadn't minded the extra hand-holding going on, either.

They walked side by side toward the guy Madison had pointed out. He was a large man with a loud voice and what appeared to be a big personality. The second he entered the room, people surrounded him, chatting and laughing in an animated way. His wife seemed equally familiar and friendly with everyone.

Eric could almost feel Madison's hand getting cold and clammy in his. Her hold seemed to tighten as they got closer to the circle of people. At the edge, she paused, her eyes darting back and forth between Dave and everyone else.

Knowing he had nothing to lose, Eric decided to help her integrate into the group. He made a show of stutter-stepping before tripping into one of the men standing near them.

"Oh gosh, excuse me! I'm so sorry about that," he said, extending his hand to shake the other man's.

"Don't worry about it," the guy said good-naturedly, "my wife always says I have two left feet as well."

Luckily, their exchange caught the notice of the group and, specifically, the CEO.

"Madison." The loud voice Eric had heard from across the room two minutes ago was addressing them. "You made it. So glad you're here."

He stepped forward and shook Madison's hand.

At the connection, she seemed to blossom back into her confident self. "Yes, thank you again for the invitation, Dave. This party is lovely."

The man smiled and looked about him. "It is a nice venue. I wish I could say I played some part in organizing it, but I leave that to the event planners." He said this with a wink then turned to pull the woman he'd come with forward. "Let me introduce you to my wife, Liz."

The woman greeted them with a happy smile. "Good evening, it's a pleasure to meet you." She wasn't a stunning beauty, but there was something riveting about her gaze and the poised way she presented herself.

"Liz, this is Madison. She's one of the people we're interviewing for the company right now."

"Oh, how wonderful!" Her knowing eyes flitted toward Eric, and he wondered if Madison would introduce him or if he should do it himself.

"And this is my boyfriend, Ethan, I told you about." Madison's clear voice answered his question. "Ethan, this is Dave Stevens, the CEO of Sube Nutritionals."

Eric reached out to shake Dave's hand.

"Well, it's great to meet you, Ethan," Dave said as he pumped their hands. "As I told Madison the other day, we are definitely a family company here. We love meeting the important people in our employees' lives."

Eric wanted to laugh at how quickly his status had jumped from pretend boyfriend to family. "I'm happy to meet you as well. Madison has said so many good things about everyone."

Madison glanced back at him, and the bright smile she gave was one hundred percent genuine. Suddenly, he really did feel like Prince Charming, ready and willing to do anything to make his Cinderella happy. Or at least to make her smile like that at him again.

Dave got tapped on the shoulder by someone and was momentarily distracted. After a few brief words, he turned back. "I have to take care of something, but we need to talk some more. Make sure you're seated at our table when the dinner starts." He motioned to his wife. "If I get there late, make sure these two are by us."

Liz nodded graciously. "Of course, I want to hear more about you both, too." She gave them a wink. "I'm a sucker for a good love story. Our kids are all grown and married, so I have no one to entertain me."

"Of course," Madison said. "Our history is pretty boring, but we love to talk about it." If Madison hadn't reached up and began twirling her hair, Eric might've almost believed her statement.

He reached for her hand before it got too tangled up and kissed the back of it. "I'm sure we can rustle up some good dirt on each other."

Liz's eyes danced between the two of them. "I'm sure you can," was all she said.

Chapter 7

The night had only been going on for about an hour and already it felt like an eternity. Madison's emotions had jumped from high to low, from confident to uncertain, and everything in between.

Was she a good fit for this company? Of course she was. But was she even qualified for this position? What if she got it and totally screwed everything up? Of course she wouldn't—she was top of her class. This is what she trained the last six years for. Right?

Only the constant presence of Eric seemed to pull her out of the swirling vortex of doubts during the night. He seemed to know exactly what to say every time.

How had they only known each other for twenty-four hours? It felt like so much longer. Pretending they were dating had been awkward for the first little bit, but now it seemed like reality. Remembering his name was "Ethan" instead of Eric proved to be one of the hardest parts.

The cocktails and mingling lasted another twenty minutes before someone got up in front and asked people to start seating themselves.

Madison had been keeping an eye on Liz to see which table she headed for. It appeared that they were sitting in the center, near the front.

Eric must have noticed as well, because he wordlessly led Madison in that direction.

When they reached the table, Liz was seated and talking with the woman across from her. She glanced up and noticed Madison and Eric.

"Come, come. Grab a seat before they're all snatched up," she said, standing and waving her arms at them.

Madison noted where Liz had placed her purse. She was obviously saving a spot for her husband, so Madison made sure to sit in the chair next to it. If she wanted to make the most of this night, she better get in some good conversations with Dave. Eric pulled out her chair, then seated himself.

While Liz and the other woman continued their conversation, Eric tilted his head toward her. "So, what do you think they're serving for dinner?"

She turned toward him. "I bet it's something healthy."

His face fell in an exaggerated motion, the hollow of his cheeks creating the perfect picture of disappointment. "So, you're telling me we're not going to get deep dish pizza?"

She almost laughed out loud. "If I was a betting woman, I'd assume there'd be some sort of salad followed by a lean meat and side."

"I've changed my mind; I don't think I want you working for a health company. I think it will have bad effects on our relationship if all your work events are so nutritionally conscious," he said, inspecting the white napkin on his plate folded to look like a rose.

"I think it's just something you're going to have to suffer through. Because I don't know if you realize this,"—Madison cocked her head—"but I studied dietetics. Any company I work for would be health conscious."

"The things I do for you," he mumbled, but she didn't miss the glint of humor in his eyes.

Madison pretended not to be affected by the meaningless banter, but inside, her thoughts were swirling. Why did he speak as if they were going to have a relationship after this? They both knew this whole boyfriend-girlfriend thing was all a fraud. Was he just having fun flirting? Or was he actually hinting at his real feelings?

She pushed the questions aside, not having the mental energy to dwell on them at the moment.

The room had slowly begun settling. Most of the tables were full, including their own. An older couple sat to Eric's left, and the woman Liz had been talking to was joined by her date. Finally, even Dave joined them.

Relief hit Madison that there didn't seem to be any other job applicants at their table. In the back of her mind, she was afraid Dave had asked all the potential candidates to sit with him tonight.

An MC stood at the front of the room and gathered everyone's attention again. "Welcome, welcome, everyone..." The man's deep voice went on to explain the evening. They would start with dinner. While everyone was served, a short presentation would be given on what the charity organization had accomplished in the past year. Once everyone had eaten, the auction would begin, followed by a brief concluding speaker.

When the man sat down, Dave turned to Madison and Eric, an eager look in his gaze. "So, I want to hear more about you two. Madison gave me a good history on herself, but tell me about how Ethan fits in the picture."

Madison's voice caught in her throat, and she suddenly couldn't remember a single part of the made up history they had agreed upon.

Eric placed a warm hand on her knee under the table. "Half the time I don't know where I fit in, either. Madison runs the show most days."

This earned him a loud laugh from Dave.

Eric continued, giving her another moment to collect her thoughts. "Let's see, Madison and I have been dating about a year now. Right, hon?"

She nodded, the motion swinging her earrings haphazardly about her face.

"We met through a mutual friend. She gave me Madison's number, but after seeing her picture, I couldn't quite get up the guts to call her for a while." He pulled at his collar in an exaggerated motion, earning him some laughs from their companions.

"Women never will understand the pain men go through asking them out on that first date," Dave agreed as he put his arm around his wife.

"Psh! You men have no idea the pain *women* go through to get ready for that first date," Liz retorted. "And every date after. I spent almost forty-five minutes on my hair alone tonight."

"And you look stunning for it," Dave replied without a second's pause.

At this point, Madison figured she had better take the reins. It was her, after all, not Eric, that needed to leave a good impression. "Yes, and when Ethan finally did ask me, I was quite surprised by his choice of activity."

She gave a humorous summary of their fictitious first date at an arcade.

Liz clearly loved every detail. "Oh, honey, I totally get you. Dave thought it would be a great idea to have me over for a family dinner on our first date. With his parents and *everything*." She rolled her eyes dramatically. "Talk about awkward."

"It's a good thing I'm so handsome. Otherwise, there's no way you would've gone on a second date with me," Dave said, giving his wife a peck on the cheek.

They talked a bit more about funny dating stories. The couple on the other side of Eric had a great one about a time the husband took his wife fishing and ended up capsizing the boat.

When things began to die down, Liz turned back to Madison. "So, you guys have been together for a year now. I'm assuming you've met each other's families and such?"

"Uh, yeah. Of course." Madison only stumbled for a second. "I'm especially close with his sister." She smiled, thinking how April would have snickered at that answer.

"So, do you guys have any future plans?"

The question took Madison by surprise. She was prepared to answer questions about their past; she didn't realize they'd get questions about their future. "Oh, um... Well, we're just taking things one day at a time right now."

Dave cut in. "Liz, leave them alone." He turned to Madison. "Liz loves nothing more than weaseling details out of everyone about their love lives."

Liz scrunched up her nose and seemed about to add something when the lights dimmed. A second later, a video began playing on the large screen, and Madison let out a silent sigh of relief.

The video was very well done. It explained the process of how the charity helped communities with poor nutritional knowledge and resources. The focus of it all was mostly children—a topic that hit Madison's heart. The thought of young kids going without proper food was so sad. She would be proud to work for a company that supported organizations like this one.

The video lasted about twenty minutes, during which the waiters served everyone a bright-green spinach salad consisting of goat cheese, berries, and some sort of candied nuts. Next, came an assortment of roasted root veggies along with strips of perfectly grilled steak.

"This actually looks pretty good," Eric whispered, elbowing her. He buttered a roll as he spoke, the yeasty scent filling Madison's nose. "Maybe I'll let you work for this company after all."

"And maybe I'll get you to start eating vegetables more regularly," was her reply. She was almost embarrassed at how much she loved his teasing. It brought her back to grade school days where being one of the kids in on the joke was the ultimate compliment. She felt a faint blush creeping up her neck, and she tried to focus on cutting her steak.

As everyone continued eating, the MC stood up again. "I hope you all enjoyed that wonderful presentation. As you can see, this work is changing the lives of the next generation. With that in mind, let's begin the next portion of the evening, the auction!"

He proceeded to explain how the bidding would work and what types of items would be up for sale. They started off with a five-day, all-inclusive trip to Hawaii. The bidding was rapidfire, and everyone had fun seeing the different items going up. Some were large, extravagant vacation trips; others were smaller items like local event tickets or gift cards.

Madison wasn't surprised when Dave and his wife purchased one or two items. It would be appropriate for them to set a good example. She *was* surprised, though, when Eric got in on the action. He first put in for some gift cards to a local restaurant but got outbid quickly. He finally found success at bidding on two tickets to an opera show in a couple months.

After the MC confirmed he'd won the item, Liz leaned over. "I didn't realize you were so musically inclined. I love opera as well. I'm sure it will be a wonderful show."

When she turned her attention back to the bidding, Madison leaned close and whispered, "The opera, huh?"

Eric shrugged. "What can I say? I'm cultured." After another second, he quietly added, "And I may or may not have thought the guy said they were Oprah tickets. Isn't she a talk host girls love?"

Madison had to hide her snort with a napkin. "You—you thought they were Oprah tickets?"

The corner of Eric's mouth crept up. "Yeah, I don't know. I thought maybe you'd like to go with me to it or something."

Madison just shook her head, smiling. "Well, first off, Oprah's talk show ended several years ago, but also, how are you planning on going to that when you'll be in Boston?"

Eric just shrugged his shoulders. "I don't know, we'll figure something out." He grinned before shoving a giant bite of potatoes in his mouth.

We'll? Madison thought to herself.

The auction lasted a bit longer, during which the waiters brought everybody a slice of a three-layer dark chocolate cake. Madison couldn't help noticing how quickly Eric inhaled it. She secretly loved that he had a sweet tooth. Being in the nutrition industry sometimes surrounded her with people that were a little stuffy when it came to their food. It was refreshing to see someone simply enjoy a meal without questioning its nutritional value.

Once the betting ended, the final speaker got up. The woman was the executive director of the charity and got extremely emotional while thanking everyone for their donations that night. Her heart was clearly in it.

Everyone clapped when she finished, and the noise in the room escalated as people began mingling again.

"This evening has been wonderful. I'm so glad we came," Madison said to Dave and Liz as they all stood from the table.

"It really is an amazing organization. We've been supporting them for about four years now, and I've loved working with them," he replied.

Surprisingly, Eric piped in from behind her. "So, how involved are you guys with the actual work they do?"

Dave lifted one shoulder. "I wish we could do more. Obviously, we financially back them. About twice a year, we get together and do some sort of service project." His face brightened. "This year, we're actually doing a little two-day retreat. We'll be spending two full days packing supplies to send down to Mexico." He narrowed his eyes. "The retreat is actually at the end of this month, in about two weeks. We're looking for more to join if you're interested."

As much as Madison liked the charity and the work they were doing, she knew she'd have to refuse. Eric would be in Boston, and there was no way she could come up with a good enough cover story for why he wasn't there.

"If only—"

"We'd love to."

It took all her energy not to betray her shock at Eric's confident reply. Instead, she formed her mouth into a smile and said, "Ethan's right. That would be a great opportunity." She glanced over her shoulder at him, making sure she'd understood correctly. His quick nod left her no doubt. "You're sure you'll have space for both of us?"

Dave's wide smile was becoming a familiar sight. "Of course! I'm so happy you can come. It's going to be a wonderful weekend."

Liz tapped Dave's shoulder and motioned to the other side of the room. "I think a few of the board donors want to speak with you."

Dave looked to where she pointed and nodded his head. He turned back to Madison and Eric. "I hate to run, but I've got to go schmooze with some folks. It's been a pleasure spending the evening with you." He offered a hand to Madison. "How about we talk again in my office on Monday morning? Say 9 AM?"

Madison nodded, too nervous that if she opened her mouth, she might squeal with glee.

Dave offered his hand to Eric next. "Ethan, I'm glad to have met you. You two seem like a dynamic pair."

Eric shook his hand and grinned. "What can I say, Madison keeps me on my toes."

Liz waved goodbye, then she and Dave were off, mingling through the crowd.

Madison let out the breath she'd been holding, suddenly exhausted.

Eric put his arm around her and let her lean into him, the simple intimacy so natural after a few hours of pretending.

"You did great tonight," he said to the top of her head.

Madison snorted. "I don't know if I'd say that...but I think my odds are pretty good if Dave wants to meet with me Monday morning."

She could feel Eric nodding.

"You ready to go?" he asked after another minute.

"Yeah." She stepped away from him and grabbed her clutch off of the table. "Let's go."

Fifteen minutes later, they were safely stowed in his car, the smooth leather seats and dark interior a welcome relief to Madison's frazzled nerves. Good thing she never pursued an acting career—it was clearly not for her.

They drove in silence, each of them lost in their own thoughts. Madison's mind roved through all the conversations she'd had, finally settling on Eric's agreement to attend the humanitarian retreat in a few weeks. Why had he done that? It would be a total inconvenience if he actually planned on attending.

"So, I have to ask. Why did you agree to go to that retreat Dave spoke about?" She smoothed the silky fabric of her dress as she spoke.

Eric didn't answer for a second. "I don't know, I guess the presentation really hit me hard." He ran his free hand through his hair, mussing the dark strands slightly. "Let's just say, I could probably use a little bit more selflessness in my life."

Madison wanted to ask what he meant but didn't want to seem nosy.

"I mean, I make plenty of money," he luckily continued. "Probably too much for a single guy to need. I'm at the point where I'm tired of just thinking about myself. It's always all about me. My work, my comfort... I live such an isolated life that I very rarely think of or help others."

He laughed lightly, and Madison realized the conversation made him uncomfortable.

"Anyway, it just hit me that this would be a good thing to do with my time. A good way to think of others instead of myself for a couple of days." He looked over at her and reached for her hand, squeezing it lightly before dropping it again. "Sorry I roped you into it."

Madison tried to pretend she didn't miss the warmth of his palm. "No, it's fine. I loved the presentation as well. It'll be good to get involved." She leaned back into the chair, enjoying the feeling of having nothing to do for the moment. "We'll figure it out when the time comes."

Inside, though, her thoughts were still running. Would this prolong their "fake relationship"? Eric planned on staying at their apartment for at least another week, maybe two. Would they continue hanging out and spending time with each other, or would Eric simply remain as a houseguest?

The thought of hanging out with Eric wasn't an unwelcome one. Every moment she had spent in his company had been fun and enjoyable. But she was also leery of him, as well. Madison wasn't sure if she could continue spending time around him without developing feelings. She might've already begun to, if she was being honest with herself.

She also worried about having to play the pretend girlfriend in front of her future coworkers for two full days. Tonight had been one thing—anybody could pretend for a couple of hours—but a whole weekend?

She sighed and snuggled against the window pane. No use in brooding over it. The evening had been a success, and for that, she gave thanks.

*****

Eric watched as Madison shifted in her seat, the intricate beading of her dress reflecting bits of light from the passing cars.

Good thing he drove. Otherwise, he'd have had a hard time keeping his eyes off of her. Madison presented herself in such a confident, classy way. He had dated lots of attractive girls over the years, but she seemed to be in a league of her own. Spending the evening as her boyfriend had been no problem at all.

He mentally shook his head and reminded himself that this was just a weekend gig. Madison simply needed a man to stand in for her; she didn't really have feelings for him. They'd only known each other for a day, for crying out loud. And ultimately, he'd be gone in two weeks or less. No point in starting something.

Eric saw Madison move again and wondered what she was thinking. He hoped she wasn't too upset about him agreeing to go on the retreat. It had kind of been an impulse move. It was just hard to think people could live with so little and not want to help in some way.

He might've had an underlying ulterior motive as well. The retreat would give him two solid days of hanging out with Madison.

Simply as a friend, of course.

When they got back to her apartment, she hopped out before he could get around to her side. He trailed her to the front door, simultaneously lamenting and grateful that they were both going in—forgoing any tension-filled door scene. And the fact that April lounged on the couch when they walked in killed any romantic mood as well.

Madison turned toward him before heading for her bedroom. "Really, thanks again for tonight, Eric. You were perfect. I think half the reason Dave might hire me is because he liked you so much."

"What can I say, there's a lot to love about me," Eric said, throwing his head back dramatically. What he'd really wanted to say was he'd do anything to help her; she deserved the best.

She smiled, her eyes half closed. Waving to April, she simply said, "All right, I'm beat. Good night."

Then, it was just April and Eric left. April looked up from her phone she'd been scrolling through. "*So*...how was the night with your girlfriend?"

Eric covered his eyes and shook his head. "I'm going to brush my teeth then go to bed. So you better scoot your bum off that couch before I get back."

She wiggled her eyebrows at him. "That good, huh?"

He just sighed as he left the room.

Chapter 8

This was probably one of the best Mondays in Madison's life.

She'd met with Dave that morning, and as hoped, he'd offered her the job. She'd been on cloud nine ever since.

The next two hours were spent with HR, going over paperwork, health insurance, and all the other boring stuff that had to get done. From then on, she'd been shadowing some of the other food scientists in the office.

The only reason she allowed herself to take a lunch break was because she wanted to call everyone and tell them the good news.

As she stepped out of the elevator on the first floor, she pulled out her phone. She shocked herself when the first number she dialed was Eric's. As she heard the ring go off, she almost hung up. But then, his deep voice answered.

"Hello?"

"Hey, Eric, it's me. Madison." She knew her words were a little stilted. He probably wondered why the heck she was calling him. A burst of pleasure shot through her at his response, though.

"Mads, I've been waiting to hear from you. How'd it go? Did you get the job?"

Even though he couldn't see her, Madison broke into a wide smile. That shortened version of her name felt so personal coming from him. "Yes," she cried. "I got it! I've been shadowing people all morning, and it's so fascinating." Instead of making her way to her car, she sat on a park bench outside the office. The next five minutes were spent describing everything from that morning. Eric listened with a patient ear, never once hurrying her on.

When she finished describing the lab results she'd analyzed a few minutes ago, he said, "That's awesome, way to go. I mean, clearly I knew you'd get the job, but still, good for you." His excitement mirrored hers. "What are we doing to celebrate?"

She loved the way he said *we*, like he was an integral part of her life. Running her fingers along the metal armrest, she answered, "I don't know, I haven't really thought that far."

"I'll talk with April, and we'll take you somewhere good tonight." He paused before adding, "Although, I can't promise it'll be healthy."

Madison laughed, scaring the flock of pigeons that had slowly been circling her, hoping for some scraps of food. "All right, I'll plan on it. Thanks again for all your help with this."

"No problem, you did all the work. I was just the extremely attractive trophy boyfriend that everyone loved, after all."

"Don't forget humble. The humble, attractive trophy boyfriend that everyone loved," she said without missing a beat.

He laughed into the phone, giving her a burst of satisfaction before saying goodbye.

She stared down at her now dark phone in her hands. What was it about Eric that made her feel so good? Every time she talked to him, the day seemed a little brighter and a little happier.

She knew April was in the middle of teaching a class, so she just sent her a text with the exciting news. She'd call her parents later tonight to tell them about the job as well. Eyeing the birds once again approaching her, she decided to go get herself something to eat.

She checked her watch and saw she had thirty minutes. Plenty of time to go grab a sandwich or something. But honestly, she couldn't wait to get back to her new position.

*****

When Madison walked in her apartment door at 5:30 that afternoon, a gorgeous bouquet sitting on the countertop greeted her. An array of pale lilies mixed with what she thought were chrysanthemums in a bright pink were framed by leafy greens. An attached card read *Congratulations!*

"Hey, hey, look who's here," Eric's voice echoed from the couch, and a second later, she saw him stand and walk toward her.

She looked at the flowers then back at him. "Did you get these?" she asked, not even trying to hide the surprise in her voice.

He stopped a few feet from her and shoved his hands in his pockets. "Yeah, you know, it's kind of a big deal to get your dream job. I figured a congratulatory bouquet was in order." He shifted his weight from one socked foot to the other.

She couldn't remember the last time someone had bought her flowers. The thoughtfulness of the gesture struck her. "That was so nice of you. Thank you!" She shocked herself by stepping forward with her arms outstretched.

He received her hug without hesitation. If anything, he seemed to hang on a second longer than necessary.

"You ready for dinner?" he asked as he stepped back. "We have about ten minutes before we have to leave to meet April at what she claims is the 'best Indian restaurant ever.'"

"You guys really don't need to take me to dinner," she said, her keys making a slight clattering noise as she set them on the countertop.

"Sure we do. Besides, pretty soon you'll be making more than both of us and paying for our meals when we go out."

She rolled her eyes. "Ten minutes, you say? I'd better put on my stretchy pants if we're getting Indian."

He smiled and moved aside so she could walk by.

As she passed the living room, she noticed her perfectly arranged bookshelf seemed slightly off. Nothing major, just a few books randomly placed. Huh, she'd need to remember to fix that when she got back tonight.

When they walked out the door a few minutes later, Madison wore her favorite pair of fitted jeans and a slim-cut black top as opposed to the stretchy pants she claimed to be changing into. Normally, she'd go with flats, but tonight she picked out a pair of ankle boots, the three-inch heel doing wonders to lengthen her legs. Not that she was trying to look especially good for anyone or anything, she reminded herself. It was just a special occasion.

"Alright, I already put the address in my phone; you just tell me where to go," Eric said, handing her his cell.

She hadn't missed the second glance he'd sent her way when she'd stepped out of her room. She'd made a good call on the heels. She took the phone and followed him out to his car. She knew the sleek black sedan was just his rental for the week, but she thought it fit him.

He opened the passenger door for her, his hand on the small of her back, helping her in. Despite her pleasure at the gesture, it hinted at a more serious relationship between them. Something she needed to avoid.

What could she have done, though? Ask him to stop being so courteous? She shook her head at her own thought. She needed to just relax. Enjoy the evening. April would be with them the whole night, anyway. It wasn't going to be an intimate dinner or anything.

Once Eric got in and pulled the car out, she spent her energy giving him directions to the place. "Okay, you're going to turn left at the next intersection," she said. The phone suddenly buzzed in her hand. "Hmm, you have a new text from April. You want me to read it?"

"Sure, go ahead."

Madison scanned the message, the contents making her confidence falter slightly. "She said one of the other personal trainers called in sick, so she has to cover a client for them. She'll meet us for dessert but can't make it to dinner."

"Ah, that's a bummer." Eric gave her a side eye. "Are you fine going with just me? It might not be as fun."

She locked her teeth in a determined smile. "Of course I'm fine." As long as he didn't gaze at her with that intense expression she couldn't quite read. Turning her own eyes to the window, she added, "I'm sure you'll keep me plenty entertained."

He just laughed.

*****

The restaurant was busy, especially considering it was a Monday night. So the fact that they were seated within five minutes pleasantly surprised Eric.

"Are you a fan of Indian food?" Madison asked as she flipped through the menu.

"Sure," he shrugged, his eye catching on the large selection of curries. "I mean, to be honest, there's very few cuisines out there I don't like. I'm a pretty easy critic." Basically, anything was a step up from frozen burritos.

"So, you're saying I shouldn't be super proud that you liked my eggs the other day?"

Her question made him grin. "No, those were definitely five stars. I'm surprised you haven't opened your own restaurant."

Madison raised her eyebrows but said nothing more.

She looked good this evening. Her dark jeans fit her almost a little too perfectly. The black top she wore drew his mind back to the image of her coming in from biking, dressed all in black spandex. Now that had been an image worth remembering.

She tapped her menu lightly on the table, pulling him from his memories. "Have you ever been here before? Do you know what's good?"

Eric shook his head. "Nope. April's never brought you here?"

"No, she must have been hiding this gem from me." She ran her finger down the menu. "However, as a general rule, I always order Tikka Masala from any Indian restaurant. It's never failed me yet."

"Hmm…" Eric went back to scanning his menu. "How do you feel about sharing?" He knew some people weren't into it, better to feel her out before making suggestions.

"I'm good with it. What are you looking at?" she asked from behind the laminated sheet.

"Well, I feel morally obligated to try at least one of the curries...and then of course we have to try a kebab or two...we'll definitely need an order of their naan bread..." He'd missed lunch today, so just about everything looked good.

"You do remember that April's not coming, right? It's just you and me."

He gave her the side eye. "Madison, I am a man with a hearty appetite. Trust me, anything you can't finish, I will." He went back to his perusing, almost missing the head shake Madison sent his way.

When the waiter finally came around again, he let Madison speak up first. "I'm going to have an order of your chicken Tikka Masala, and he…"—she glanced at him with raised eyebrows—"is probably about to order way too much."

He smiled as he closed his menu. It was fun being with a woman who could keep up with his humor. After a discussion with the waiter about the different heat levels of the curries and if the fish or pork kebabs were better, he managed to limit himself to three kebabs and a yellow curry. The garlic naan wasn't up for debate, though.

Madison just cocked her head in question as the waiter left.

"Come on, Madison, we're celebrating! Isn't this why you were supposed to wear your stretchy pants?" he asked, pretending to eye her jeans with concern.

"I guess I should have worn them. But I don't know if even they could stretch enough for all the food you've ordered."

"We'll just have to bring the leftovers to April—if there are any, of course."

She laughed lightly, and his pulse seemed to accelerate at the sound. Or maybe it was the way her eyes danced on him as she smiled. Why did she have that impact on him? He had never gotten these nerves with other girls.

She interrupted his thoughts. "So, we've been so focused on my career the last couple of days. I want to hear more about *your* job for once. What got you started in it, why do you keep the schedule you do, what companies do you work for?" She listed off her questions on her fingers. "Spill it."

While he wasn't super excited to talk about work, it would be good to get the conversation and his mind to a nice, safe topic. "My job...wow, we must really have nothing to talk about if we're talking about my job," he said, one corner of his mouth lifting.

"It's interesting to me. What did you study in school?"

"Surprise, I studied computer science in college. I know,"—he lifted his hands up defensively—"it wasn't what you were thinking, but the esthetician school didn't accept my application, so I had to default to my second choice."

Madison swatted him on the arm. "Will you be serious for a second? So, you studied computer science. What did you do after school?"

"From there, I immediately got a job with a data sourcing company." He shrugged, remembering the cramped cubicle and dowdy office. "I only worked there for about a year. I didn't like it much. Too boring."

Madison sipped her water slowly as she listened.

"After that, I jumped around to one or two software companies, never really loving anything but always learning and making more connections at each location. Eventually, I got my first freelance gig about three years out of college. It was a huge contract for me at that point. They offered me the same amount of money I made in a year for about three months of work." He fiddled with the wrapper from his straw. "Needless to say, I jumped at the opportunity. I've never looked back since."

Madison silently spun her water glass, almost as if stalling. "So, do you like this way of life?" she finally asked.

"What, freelancing?"

"Well, yeah, freelancing. But the whole jumping around from place to place every few months. Not really ever having somewhere to call home?" Madison's words trailed off, her eyes darting away from his.

Eric took a deep breath and leaned back in the slightly cushioned chair. So that's what she was digging at. The constant moving. "Sometimes. When I first started, I actually loved it. It was fun living in a new place every few months. I got to see so many cities that I never would have otherwise." He tossed the crumpled straw wrapper back onto the table, reflecting on his past. It *had* been exciting for the first bit. He wished he could say it still felt that way. "I'd be lying, though, if I said it wasn't starting to get to me. The idea of doing this for a few more years—never settling down or putting roots anywhere—does seem a little dismal."

Madison leaned forward and rested her elbows on the table.

Eric didn't normally open up to people, but something about the way those soft eyes studied his face got him talking. "I think one of my main problems is that I don't know how to do it. Where or when do I stop? Should I settle back in Colorado again? Should I try somewhere new? I have so many connections at this point that I could probably find a job anywhere. It's just making that decision."

"Do you have anyone—"

"All right, I have one order of Tikka Masala..." Their waiter returned with arms full of steaming plates.

Eric sighed, equally grateful and frustrated for the interruption. He had been getting way too personal. As a general rule, he never went past surface level with women. Why could Madison pull things out of him so easily?

"Can I get you anything else?" the waiter asked with a friendly smile. The scent of exotic spices and flavors wafted from the warm food in front of them.

"I think we'll be good for a while," Eric replied, sending a wink toward Madison.

The waiter nodded and turned back toward the kitchen.

They rotated the plates between them like a carousel, never lingering on one dish too long. More than once, their hands bumped, often of Eric's own doing. Undeniable waves of attraction pulsed through him. Did she feel it too?

Focusing on the food helped. The yellow curry with its chunks of seasoned meat and potatoes was heaven, but the chicken was delicious, too. It amazed him how much flavor they managed to pack into an inch of meat. And despite Madison's protests, she ate her fair share of everything, even including the chewy naan bread.

Fifteen minutes later, she leaned back from her plate. "Oh my gosh, my stomach is going to explode."

Eric was still going strong with the kebabs and rice. "Just take a three-minute breather," he said, sliding a saucy cube of meat off the stick, "then you can come back in for more."

"I don't think I'm going to fit in your car if I keep eating."

He laughed. "C'mon, Mads, where's your stamina?"

She grinned, but her smile slowly dimmed to an uncertain look. "Back to our earlier discussion…" She studied her fingernails, no longer looking him in the eye. "Do you have anyone that would draw you to a certain location?"

Eric looked up from the now-empty stick he held. "What?" Had he heard her right?

A red flush crept up her cheeks as she took a quick sip of water. "I just asked if there was anyone...um, special, I guess...that would make you want to settle down somewhere specific." Despite her claim to be stuffed, she grabbed the flatbread she'd deserted on her plate and took a giant bite.

"Oh, anyone special, hmm..." Eric tapped the side of his head with his stick, pretending to think. He kind of liked this flustered version of Madison. It proved she wasn't feeling as confident as she looked. "I mean, there was this one guy that lived in the apartment next to me in Dallas that still owes me fifty bucks. So, I could move back there in hopes of getting that one day." He tossed the empty kebab on his plate. He knew she was fishing for information, but he wasn't going to give it out that easily.

Madison sneaked a quick glance at him then back down. "Oh, well, I guess the sky's the limit then." She shoved another piece of bread in her mouth.

He took a sip of water, the ice clinking in the cup as it moved. He decided to turn the pressure onto her. "How about you? Any particular reason—or person—you decided to stick around Colorado for?"

Madison shrugged. "Sube Nutritionals was definitely a draw. But my family is close, too. My parents live about two hours away, and my brothers are both in the city here."

"Oh yeah? You never told me anything about your family. You say you have two brothers?"

"Yeah, they're both older than me. One of them got married last year—quite the fiasco, but it all worked out.

The other is still single. Then, my parents live south, toward Colorado Springs area."

Eric nodded, noticing she hadn't mentioned any romantic connections. "So, just family, huh? No one else keeping you here?"

She glanced at him sharply. "Well, there's always April. I couldn't leave her."

"She is a pretty helpless thing, isn't she? No boyf—"

Just then, Eric's phone started ringing. He pulled it out and looked at the screen. Putting it to his ear, he said, "April, speak of the devil. What's up, my little workaholic?"

"Very funny," his sister's voice said over the line. "You're definitely not one to talk, Mr. Works the Graveyard Shift."

Eric could see Madison eyeing him curiously. "You off the clock?"

April sighed. "Yeah, finally. I've got to stop being so nice to people. Are you guys finished eating? There's a yogurt shop just down the street from you if you're ready for dessert."

Eric felt stuffed, but he figured yogurt could slide through the cracks. "That sounds good, we'll plan on it."

"Cool, see you in about ten minutes. Oh, and bring me your leftovers."

"What makes you think we have any?"

"Trust me, I've eaten there before. Each of their servings are enough to feed three people."

He eyed the remains of their meal and had to agree with her. After he hung up, he turned to Madison. "April's off of work. She suggested meeting at some yogurt shop just down the street."

Madison reached up in a stretch. "Okay, although, I don't know how much frozen yogurt I can eat. I can barely breathe as it is."

He looked down at their plates. They'd probably be coming home with as much food as they'd eaten. "We're going to need a box for all this," he said. "April left me explicit instructions to bring her the leftovers."

"Ha ha, yes, sir," Madison said with a salute.

*****

Madison leaned back in the chair at her new desk the next day. She had put in a solid morning getting to know more of what would be expected of her at Sube, and a lunch break sounded perfect. She should probably grab something healthy like a salad after last night's indulgence.

Getting yogurt had been fun. Eric and April sang a very off-key version of "For She's a Jolly Good Fellow," and Madison ate way too much, but it'd been the perfect cap to the night.

There was only one awkward moment. The time Eric had reached for her hand when they were waiting in line, and April exclaimed she felt like a third wheel.

Eric immediately defended his actions by claiming he'd gotten the habit from their dinner on Saturday night. April hadn't seemed convinced, though.

The whole situation just flustered Madison. Honestly, his hand grab *had* felt natural, even though she knew it shouldn't have. They'd only known each other for a few days. So, why did it seem so much longer?

She snapped out of her daydream when her phone started ringing. April's name flashed across the screen.

Madison wasn't surprised. They had all gone straight to bed last night, so there had been no girl talk. April clearly wanted some answers. She hit the green answer button and brought the device to her ear.

"Hi, April, what's up?" She knew her voice sounded too peppy.

"Eh, nothing, just getting out of class."

Madison could hear her heavy breathing. "Must have been a hard one."

"Haha, that's usually my goal. Are you at work right now?"

"Just leaving for lunch, I can chat." She grabbed her handbag from under the desk and made her way toward the door.

"All right, girl, spill it. What's going on between you and my brother?" April's voice took on a no-nonsense tone.

"What do you mean what's going on?" Reaching the bottom of the stairs, she shoved the oversized glass door with her shoulder, finally budging it after a second. "Nothing is going on. I mean, Eric did a great job playing my boyfriend on Saturday night, but other than that, we're just friends."

"C'mon, Mads. You guys looked like more than friends to me last night. What was with all the hand-holding and batting your eyes at each other?"

Madison tried to blame the heat flooding her face on the warm sun that hit her as she made her way through the parking lot. "What are you talking about? There was one time Eric reached for my hand that you made such a big deal of. Although, that place was so packed last night it was no wonder. We were just squeezed right up next to each other." Madison didn't know why she defended Eric's actions so adamantly.

"I didn't see him grabbing *my* hand."

"You're his sister. That would be weird."

"It should probably be weird to grab a friend's hand, too, don't you think?"

Madison ignored the question and moved on to April's next accusation. "And I never once batted my eyes at him."

"I don't know, there seemed to be some long looks between the two of you."

Madison pulled out her keys as she reached her car. Obviously, her complete denials weren't convincing her friend. "All right, you want to know the truth? I may have a *tiny*, little crush on your brother." April and her had always been each other's confidant when it came to men. It was basically the golden rule of being roommates. But for some reason, the fact that Eric was April's brother made the whole thing a little awkward.

Opening her door, she slid into the driver's seat, momentarily soaking in the heat from the sunbaked car. "He's a cute guy. He's nice and funny. Any girl would have the same reaction."

Madison didn't add that her feelings for him were beginning to get a lot stronger than they would for a normal crush. "I am well aware that he is not here long term. I know he's going to pack up and leave in a week and be out of my life. So, I have absolutely zero expectations in terms of this going anywhere or becoming anything."

There, that explanation ought to appease April.

April stayed silent for a moment. "Well, I can't say I'm surprised."

"What do you mean?"

"I have to be honest, I actually had hopes of something sparking between you two."

"Oh no, were you trying to set us up?" Madison abhorred being set up by others.

"No! No, I honestly wasn't. Pinky promise. I just thought there was a chance you two might hit it off, was all. I mean, I know you both better than anyone, and your personalities would be perfect for each other."

Madison couldn't argue with her on that point. She and Eric did have a great time whenever they were together.

April was still talking. "It's not that I want you to get together. Sometimes, I just think that Eric needs a different lifestyle. It's not good for him to always be jumping around from one place to another, never settling down. Sometimes, I don't even think *he* likes it. But I don't know if he'll ever change unless he finds a reason to."

Madison felt the weight in her roommate's statement. "And you think I could be his reason?"

"Not unless you think so."

Chapter 9

The next couple days fell into a steady rhythm at Madison's work. It would take her at least a month to learn all the systems and processes the company used. But every day, she caught on a little more.

She wasn't exactly sure what Eric did with his time all day. He was just stirring when she walked out the door in the mornings, but when she got home on Tuesday, he wasn't around and didn't return until late.

Had he been out with someone? Was he meeting an old fling? She tried to remind herself that he was a grown man and surely had plenty of friends he'd acquired over the years. Friends he was probably just catching up with.

She couldn't totally erase her jealous curiosity, though.

However, when she walked in the door Wednesday night, Eric stood waiting for her at the kitchen table. In front of him sat a small, travel-sized chess board, perfectly laid out and ready to play.

"What's this?" she asked as she set down her bag. She tried to not let her happiness at seeing him show.

"I thought it was time you shook the dust off your chess skills." Eric leaned his elbows on the table. "Plus, it's not every day you get such a worthy opponent such as myself to play against." He wiggled his eyebrows. "That is, unless you're scared."

Madison rubbed her hands together as she pulled out a chair with her foot. "Never. I accept your challenge, and I think secretly you're the one who is scared."

Eric grinned. "Excellent." He spun the board slightly so the white pieces were in front of her. "Since you say it's been a while, you can be white."

Madison lifted her chin an inch. Generally, white always went first and was thought to have a slight advantage because of it. She wasn't sure if her pride could handle the offering. But it had been at least two years since her last match, so she accepted with a nod.

"Pawn to e4," Madison declared, making her first move.

Eric grinned. "Let the games begin."

They each played quickly, the board becoming a complicated maze of black and white pieces.

"So, how was work?" Eric finally asked.

"Good. We're working on a new line of snack items that are fortified with extra nutrients. It's kind of a tricky process." She noticed the hint of stubble she'd seen on him the first night was back. He apparently only shaved a couple times a week. It gave him this raw, manly look that she couldn't help finding attractive.

"So, like vitamins in a cracker form?"

"Something like that." Madison quickly killed one of his knights with her bishop, thoroughly enjoying herself. She couldn't remember the last time she had played a game just for fun.

"Ah...I didn't even see that," Eric mumbled.

"How about you? What have you been up to the last few days?" She tried to sound casual, not like she was specifically fishing to find out where he'd been last night.

He shrugged. "Eh, nothing much. Watching TV. Working on some billing—probably my least favorite part about freelancing." He studied the board in silence before adding, "Actually, yesterday, I went out hiking. I met a couple of my old college buddies at a local trail we used to frequent back in the day. Then, we grabbed dinner afterwards. It was fun catching up with them after all these years." One corner of his mouth lifted as he killed off another of her pawns.

"You are much too cheerful every time you do that," she said, making no comment about his hiking trip. She couldn't help the happy feeling bubbling inside her at the knowledge that he hadn't been out with another girl, though.

Biting her cheek so she didn't grin like an idiot, she changed the subject. "Where did you get this game anyway? Don't tell me you travel with a chess game?"

"As a matter of fact I do." Eric leaned back and scratched the side of his head. "You never know when you might find another chess nerd."

"Haha, I'm glad I meet your standards." She chewed her lip and eyed the board, feeling like she'd missed something. Eric was too relaxed, almost as if he knew something about the game she didn't. She moved her bishop two spots over. Her hope was to draw his queen away from the king so she could put him in check.

"So, you used to play with your dad?" Eric's voice broke her concentration.

"Yeah, he taught me to play. But my brothers loved it more than me." She looked up and realized he studied her as he spoke. Self-consciously, she tucked a stray piece of hair behind her ear. She hadn't glanced in the mirror since this morning. Did she look alright?

"I used to play with my dad, too," he said, turning his heat-inducing gaze back to the board. "Although, my grandpa is the one who originally taught me to play."

"I remember April once saying your grandpa lived with you guys for a while." She kicked off her heels and folded her legs underneath her.

Eric nodded as he made his next move. "Yeah, he eventually moved to a rest home, but during most of my high school years, he lived with us. I was his regular chess partner. He taught me all his old tricks."

"Are you trying to intimidate me?" Madison narrowed her eyes, trying to keep a stern face.

Eric leaned in close. "Is it working?"

She pressed her lips together, trying to hide her smile. "Nope." Grabbing her rook, she swiftly killed off his other knight.

"Nice move," he said, "but unfortunately…" He moved his own rook across the board, quickly taking out her queen.

"What! Why you little…" Madison couldn't believe she hadn't seen that coming. She stood up from her seat. "I need a drink of water. I'm clearly not thinking straight. You want one?"

Eric still had that little grin on his face. "Sure, thank you."

She walked into the kitchen, noticing that her decorative candles were no longer on the counter. She swore they were there that morning... Shaking it off, she grabbed two cups out of the cupboard and filled them with ice. She took her time with the task, trying to mentally distance herself from this flirtatious man she was becoming way too attracted to. *He's leaving in a week,* she chided herself, taking a deep breath.

Feeling more levelheaded, she walked back to the table, the ice clinking against the glasses in her hands. As she leaned over to hand Eric his, however, her foot caught on the handbag she'd placed on the floor, and she began to fall. She slid forward, slamming the glasses on the table, trying to stop herself. Eric simultaneously lunged to catch her.

They fell in a jumbled mess of chess pieces and spilled water, and somehow, Madison ended up cradled in Eric's lap on the floor.

The burst of chaos turned to a stilled silence. The front of her jacket was soaked, and his shirt sported a few wet spots as well. But Madison was oblivious to the water as well as the pain shooting down her forearms and hip. All she could think about was the hard wall of Eric's chest, cradling her against him, and the way her hands grasped his shirt tightly, almost with a mind of their own. As her eyes moved from his chest to his face, she was mesmerized by the way his eyes were slowly scanning her own, finally landing on her mouth.

"Are—are you okay?" he finally asked, his voice low.

The words were like a lightswitch for Madison's mind. "Oh my gosh, I can't believe I did that. What a klutz." She could feel her face warm, and she pushed herself up. She swallowed hard, trying to bring some moisture back into her dry mouth.

"Are you okay? You hit pretty hard." He stood and grabbed one of her arms, flipping it over to inspect the red marks the table had made. "You'll probably have some bruising."

"The casualties of chess," Madison joked. The light tone she used did not match the rush of emotions going on inside of her. She wanted to yank her arms from Eric's grasp while simultaneously wanting him to never let go. The warmth from his fingers seeped through her skin, sending tingles up to her shoulders. He rubbed the red spot on her wrist lightly when a buzzing filled the room.

"Oh, sorry, that's my phone." Eric dropped her arms and pulled a vibrating cell out of his pocket. "Hello?" he said into the device.

Madison turned back to the table, trying to pretend she wasn't totally eavesdropping.

"Claire? How are you? Haha, what do you mean I'm a hard guy to get a hold of?" Eric's face lit up as he talked, and Madison felt her heart drop.

"Sure, I have a second to chat." He turned to Madison and held up a finger, mouthing *I'll be right back*. He slipped out the front door. "So, tell me how you've been," was the last thing Madison heard before it shut tight.

She felt so dumb. What was she doing? Why was she letting her feelings turn like this? She knew better. She knew Eric wasn't looking for anything serious. Not only because of his work life, but also because he, apparently, had other women he kept tabs on.

Grabbing a spare towel from the kitchen, she mopped up the spilled water. Luckily, neither of the glasses had broken, but their game was a lost cause. Chess pieces were scattered everywhere. She quickly gathered them up, drying any that were wet. Within a few minutes, she had cleaned up the game, nestling the pieces back into their small box.

As she set it on the table, her stomach growled noisily, her hunger just adding to the misery of the moment. Realizing she'd never eaten anything when she had gotten home, she put together a quick peanut butter and jelly sandwich and grabbed an apple. Setting her subpar meal on a plate, she headed to her room.

There was obviously no reason to wait up for Eric. Who knew how long he'd be talking to *Claire*.

*****

Madison didn't see Eric again until Friday. Work was just really busy. And she had a piled up list of errands to do, so she didn't get home until really late on Thursday.

She definitely wasn't avoiding him or anything. Definitely.

She wasn't sure why. It wasn't like Eric had done anything wrong. Mostly, she was nervous to be alone around him again. She didn't trust herself or her feelings.

Midday on Friday, though, she got a text from him.

Hey, we still need to go to the arcade together, like you promised me. I have to introduce you to the electronics of the late 80s. You free tonight?

Had she promised to go to the arcade with him? She remembered them joking about it, but she hadn't thought he was serious. She would have been lying if she said she didn't feel a burst of anticipation at the thought.

She tapped out a reply but stopped herself just before hitting send. Wait, wasn't she doing exactly what she'd promised not to do? Spending more time with him was a sure way into trouble. She looked at the response she had typed:

Sure, I don't have any plans. What time?

Almost of its own accord, her thumb hit send. Surely she could be trusted at an arcade full of teenagers, right?

His immediate response read:

When do you get off work?

I'll probably be home a little after 5:30.

Perfect, let's plan on 6ish. We'll grab something to eat while we're out too.

Something to eat? Definitely more of a date than two friends hanging out. She sent him a simple thumbs up as a response.

Putting her phone down on the desk, she noticed her palms were already a little clammy just thinking about the evening. She'd been feeling successful at putting aside her feelings for the last twenty-four hours or so, but chances were, they would all bubble to the surface tonight when she was back with Eric.

She wasn't sure if that was a good or bad thing.

*****

Eric leaned back into the couch, waiting for his internet chess opponent to make the next move.

He had been getting restless. This usually happened whenever he took a break from work. It was good to relax for a few days, but after about a week, he started getting antsy.

On Thursday, he talked to the manager of his next job to figure out his schedule. They were a manufacturing company he'd worked for before and had a good rapport with. He asked how they'd feel about him taking a few days off for the charity retreat in two weekends. They agreed that if he started the following Monday, they'd have no problem with it.

Eric was both excited and unhappy about it. He was excited to get back to work. He was unhappy because that meant leaving Madison.

A completely ridiculous sentiment.

There was nothing going on between them. At least, nothing past some light flirting. Meaningless, trivial flirting that was in no way leading to actual feelings. Eric had simply played the role of the fake boyfriend for a night. Starting a real relationship was in no way a part of the contract.

But he couldn't shake the empty feeling he got at the thought of leaving. He'd miss pretending to sleep while he listened to her rustle around before going to work. He'd miss the hurried way she'd enter the house every night when she got home. Or the way she always had to spend the first ten minutes subconsciously going through the apartment, picking things up and putting them away. She seemed ignorant to her obsession to tidiness. He'd had some fun messing with her by purposely moving objects to the wrong location. The countertop's candles got put on the coffee table; the books on her shelf got a new arrangement. So far, she hadn't seemed to notice he was the culprit.

Most of all, though, he'd miss talking with her. He loved the few times they'd been able to talk about their days when she got home. It'd been a while since he'd had such an intimate interaction with someone else. Generally, he came home from work to an empty hotel room and ate whatever takeout he'd picked up in front of the TV. Discussing daily life with someone wasn't on his schedule.

He found he kind of liked it, though.

The computer on his lap dinged, and he saw it was his turn. Almost absentmindedly, he moved his rook into a far left position. His current opponent, Chessmate322, wasn't proving to be up to the Advanced Skill level his profile claimed. Two more moves and Eric would have him in checkmate.

Pushing his computer to the side, Eric thought back to his chess game with Madison the other night. He'd been surprised when he came back and she'd already gone to bed. She must have gotten tired.

If the phone call had been anyone besides Claire, the woman who had been his virtual assistant the last four years, he wouldn't have taken it—especially if he had known it meant ending the night with Madison. But he and

Claire had been trying to get ahold of each other for a few days, so he wanted to run a few things by her.

One thing Eric was sure about, though, was he wanted to hang out with Madison one last time before leaving. His flight left for Boston on Saturday. That meant Friday night was his last opportunity.

He would make the most of it.

*****

Madison ended up getting out of work late on Friday. One of the other technicians decided to show her something in the food lab, and they lost track of time. By the time she walked out of her office it was almost 5:45. She sent Eric a text.

I'm so sorry, I'm totally late. How about I just meet you at the arcade?

His reply was prompt.

That works. See you in a few minutes.

He sent her the address of the place, and she saw it was only about ten minutes away. She checked her reflection in a compact mirror. Not bad, although her makeup could do with a little touch up. Two minutes later, she finished with a fresh coat of lip gloss and took off.

As Madison turned into the parking lot of the arcade, she immediately noticed the bright, neon signs and flashing lights coming from the dark interior. She got a flashback of a fourth grade birthday party where she spent two hours collecting tickets to buy a stuffed animal. One she probably could have gotten for about five dollars at any normal store. She shook her head at the memory.

Eric stood in front of the doors. As she stopped the car, she took a moment to admire him from afar. He looked good this evening. Unlike April had originally led her to expect, Eric actually had a decent sense of style. He tended to stick to neutral-colored crewnecks and jeans as his standard outfit. Tonight, he'd stepped it up to a gray polo but still managed to appear perfectly comfortable and laidback. She wondered, for the hundredth time, how he was still single.

She hopped out of her car, opting to leave her tailored suit jacket inside. She already felt formal enough wearing her blouse and work slacks. Her high heels clicked on the pavement as she made her way toward him.

She'd come to the ultimate decision on her way over to just enjoy the evening. Instead of stressing about smothering her attraction to Eric, she would just relax. Why not leave behind her worries for one night?

When he finally noticed her walking toward him, his face lit up with that familiar grin. "I thought you were trying to stand me up at first."

"Nah, if I really didn't want to hang out with you, I would've just said so." Madison rested a hand on her hip sassily.

"Oh, the brutally honest type. I'm not sure which is worse," he said, throwing a hand over his heart in distress.

She bit back a smile.

"All right, are you ready?" Eric asked, grabbing her hand as he headed toward the doors.

Madison almost pulled her hand out of his grasp before remembering her resolve to just enjoy the evening. Taking a calming breath, she matched him stride for stride. "Yes, I've been warming up my fingers all day for this."

He rubbed the inside of her palm with his thumb. "That's good, you're probably going to need it. I don't want to brag, but Pac-Man and Street Fighter are kind of where I shine in life."

Despite her open attitude about the night, the palm massage he gave her sent tingles down her spine.

They made their way inside the dimmed building. As Madison had seen from the outside, the place glowed with screens and monitors, all playing their cartoonish theme songs. Eric stopped at the token kiosk, getting what Madison thought was an arsenal of coins. How long did he plan on staying here?

He eyed Madison's clothes for a second before shoving all the tokens in his pockets. "I'll hold yours for you," he said, nodding toward her sleek, gray pants. "Clearly, whoever made those pants didn't think about the importance of large pockets to hold arcade tokens."

She pursed her lips. "I should've brought my fanny pack."

Eric wiggled his eyebrows. "That's a good idea. We'll have to get matching ones and wear them every time we come gaming."

Madison wanted to ask him how many more times he planned on gaming with her, but the moment was lost as he quickly walked toward one side of the room.

"Okay, okay...obviously there are some classics we need to cover, but I figure you'd need to get this out of your system first. Maybe it'll help warm you up." He stopped suddenly, and Madison realized she stood in front of a row of Skee-Ball machines.

She burst out laughing. "You don't— We don't have to—" She could barely make out the words between giggles. "You don't have to play this just for me. I know you don't consider it actually arcade-worthy."

Eric's face was solemn. "If it's important to you, it's important to me." He rested one hand over his heart. "We might just have to play a few extra rounds of Space Invaders to make up for it."

They ended up playing a solid four games of Skee-Ball each. Despite Eric's original dismay, he got into it.

"Looks like our next date is going to have to be bowling," Madison said before she realized what she had just insinuated. Who was to say there'd be another date night?

"I guess so. I definitely need to work on my form."

Madison had smoked him at the game, and he was clearly smarting from it.

He slid an arm around her back, simultaneously turning her away from the Skee-Ball machines and closer to himself. "Alright, let's go play some of the things we came for."

They spent the next half an hour making the rounds through a series of arcade games. About fifteen minutes in, Madison resigned herself to the fact that she was terrible at them all.

"How does he keep hitting me like that? I can't even get close to him," she whined, hitting the various buttons that were supposed to allow her to defend herself.

They were in the middle of her third game of Street Fighter, and so far, she'd only managed to stay alive for about thirty seconds on each round.

"Wait for it...when he comes up behind you...like that. Now hit A three times super fast, and you'll throw a ball of fire at him." As Eric spoke, he came up behind her and covered her hand hovering over the A/B buttons.

Suddenly, Madison had no idea what she was doing in terms of the video game. All she could concentrate on was the warmth coming from Eric's body and his arms around her. The fact that he spoke directly into her ear sent a stream of chills up and down her body.

"Here, like this...now hit it fast." Eric didn't seem to have the same problem as his eyes focused on the screen, his right hand tapping the buttons in rapid motion.

Unfortunately, Madison forgot her left hand was still in charge of moving the guy forward and backward, and the rather hefty sumo wrestler she was fighting managed to kill her off one more time.

As *Game Over* flashed across the screen, Eric groaned. "It's official. You're totally helpless when it comes to video games."

"Hey!" Madison said, spinning around to face him. Only then did she realize the position they were pinned in. Eric stood in front of her, one arm still resting on the machine her back was pressed up against, subsequently pinning her in place. His mouth, which had been speaking directions in her ear a moment ago, was now inches from her own.

Her gaze roved his face, moving from his lips to his penetrating blue eyes, following the hollowness of his cheeks to his jawline, and ending once again on his mouth.

And that was how they stood for what seemed like an eternity. It was probably only a few seconds, but time was irrational when it came to emotions.

"Are you two done with that machine?" a somewhat squeaky voice from behind them broke the moment.

Madison looked behind Eric to see a kid, holding a Ziploc full of tokens, shove a pair of glasses up his nose. He looked longingly at the Street Fighter game behind them.

"Oh sure, yeah, we're done with this one," Madison said, quickly stepping past Eric.

Eric smiled at the kid and stepped aside as well. "It's all yours, bud. Good luck."

The boy nodded, a serious look on his face as he set his bag of tokens down. Clearly, he planned on being there a while.

Madison saw Eric's eyes flit around the room, her own nerves mirrored in the tight way he held his brow. Even though the moment had passed, their jitters clearly hadn't.

"Well, I think we've done enough damage here. You want to grab something to eat?"

"Yeah, that'd be great," Madison replied, noting that her voice sounded about two octaves too high.

They walked outside to a dark sky, the sun having already set. "Wow, you could really lose yourself inside one of those places," Madison commented, wondering exactly how much time had passed.

Eric nodded. "I may or may not have wasted a few youthful afternoons inside the local arcade." He paused on the sidewalk and looked to the left. "There's a Mexican place just down the street. Does that sound okay? It's nothing fancy, but it's pretty good."

Madison smiled. "That's perfect. I'm starving."

Fifteen minutes later, they were seated at a vinyl table with steaming burritos in plastic wrappers sitting in front of them.

Silence flitted between them for a few minutes. Madison honestly wasn't sure what to say. She was sure there had been about a 90% chance they would've kissed in the arcade if that kid hadn't interrupted them. So what did that mean? Was something more than just a weekend flirtation going on between them? And what about Eric's other girl, Claire? Would Madison just become another name in Eric's phone after this?

"What are you thinking about?" Eric's voice stopped her cycling thoughts.

"Hm? Oh, nothing…just thinking about…work." Work. That was a safe topic, right?

"So, are you glad you went through with it?"

"With what?" Was he reading her thoughts?

"With the whole fake-boyfriend scheme. Do you think it worked out like you hoped?" Eric picked up a napkin and wiped some salsa from his fingers.

"Well, yeah. I mean, I got the job, right?" Work. They were talking about work, she reminded herself.

"But now you have to keep up with the whole fake-boyfriend thing. Are you going to make up stories about what we did over the weekends? Tell everyone the thoughtful things I did for our anniversary and all that?"

His voice had a teasing note, but the words made Madison stop cold. What *was* she going to do? It would be weird if she never talked about her boyfriend again. She would have to invent a fake breakup like she originally thought. Unless Eric had been hinting at something more. She glanced up at him. "What would you recommend?"

"You could always play off the long-distance angle. I am living in a different state for a while for work, but our love still burns strong no matter." He closed his eyes and lifted his chin in a dreamy state.

"You are ridiculous," Madison said as she threw a balled up napkin at him.

"And yet, you still love me," he answered, shoving his last bite into his mouth.

Madison rolled her eyes, struggling to conceal how much this playful banter hit home.

"You done?" Eric asked as he crinkled up his wrapper.

She waved at the last bit of her burrito she'd abandoned on her plate. "Yeah, I'm stuffed full of beans and cheese."

They walked outside and back down the street to the lot they'd parked in.

Eric followed her to her car, trailing a few feet behind as they got close. As she reached her small SUV, she turned and glanced at him. She knew she'd see him in about ten minutes at her apartment, but somehow, this felt like a goodbye scene.

"Thanks for coming with me," Eric said, rocking back on his heels. "I know video games aren't normally your thing."

Madison smiled, fiddling with a strand of hair. "I'm just sorry all your tutelage went to waste. I think I'm a lost cause."

Eric shifted so his hip leaned against her car, subsequently bringing himself within a foot of her.

This was the part where Madison should have unlocked her car and got in. But she couldn't bring herself to pull out her keys. Instead, she stalled, glancing quickly up at him,then down at her hands.

"If it makes you feel better, I think with a few more hours of practice we'll get you beating level one of Pac-Man for sure," he finally said.

Madison reached out to shove him jokingly, but he grabbed her hand and pulled her closer.
The air between them immediately changed.

She racked her brain for something to say, anything to dispel the tension. But instead, her mind filled with thoughts of how close his mouth was and how little she'd have to lean forward before they were kissing.

Eric's eyes searched hers until they turned their focus on her mouth. "Madison," he said softly, the whispered word almost a question.

All Madison's resolve left at that word. There was nothing stopping her but a few inches of oxygen. Almost in slow motion, she leaned forward, Eric meeting her halfway.

If there had ever been a *finally* moment in Madison's life, this was it. Her whole body reacted to the kiss she'd wanted all week. A tingling that started in her feet shot all the way up to her head. Any thoughts left her mind, and she was simply feeling at that point. Almost of their own accord, her arms wrapped around him, keeping him in close. His soft mouth moved as eagerly as her own, and his hands kept their strong hold on her waist.

A minute later, they pulled apart, both of their breaths coming quick.

"Gosh, I've been wanting to do that for a while," Eric said in a quiet voice, a light dancing in his eyes.

Madison bit her lip, barely holding in an energetic agreement.

They stood for a second, their foreheads resting on each other.

Eric finally broke the stillness. "So, I have something I need to tell you."

"What?" Was he going to tell her he was falling for her? Was he about to admit that he'd been developing feelings for her just like she had for him?

"I'm flying out to Boston earlier than expected. As a matter of fact, I'm leaving tomorrow."

If Madison had been looking for a sign to clarify his feelings, she got it. Her heart dropped at his words. "You're leaving already? But...I thought you were here another week?"

"I know, I was going to be. But since I'm taking days off for that retreat, I need to make up the lost time."

Madison's pulse began to pump at these words. It made perfect sense, obviously. Of course going to the charity retreat would impact his work schedule. But that didn't ease the sting of his announcement. It was almost as if he clarified that whatever this was between them, whatever this kiss had just been, it wasn't anything serious. He had his life to live, and she was simply another entertaining stop on his way.

She took a step back. The warmth from a moment ago gone.

"Well, that was impeccable timing," she finally managed to get out, wishing she could have taken back the words as soon as she'd said them. She didn't want him to know she cared. She wanted him to think she had been as unaffected by their time together as him.

Eric cocked his head. "What?"

Madison shook her head, turning to her car. "Nothing."

He stepped aside, his movements unsure. "I mean, I'll be back in two weeks, so I'll see you then?"

Madison just shrugged and pulled out her keys. A move she should've done five minutes earlier. "Whatever, yeah, I'll see you then." Madison knew her voice had an edge.

"Mads, what's wrong? Why are you mad at me?"

"I'm not mad at you. I'm not mad at anyone." She willed her voice to be nonchalant. "I'm just agreeing that we'll see each other in a couple weeks, like you said." She hit the button, and her car unlocked. Opening the driver's door, she turned to look at him one more time. "Thanks for tonight."

Eric nodded and stepped back. He obviously knew a dismissal when he heard one. "It was fun; thanks for coming." He rubbed the back of his neck. "I...I guess I'll see you at home?"

She nodded, knowing full well that she planned to go directly to her room and close the door when she got there.

"Alright, well, drive safe."

With that, she hopped inside and pulled the door shut, feeling like she closed the door on more things than just her car.

Chapter 10

Well, Eric had blown that goodbye. He shifted in his hard plastic chair, back in his home away from home: the airport terminal. His flight for Boston left in forty-five minutes, and boarding started in about twenty.

How had he messed things up so badly? He'd been trying to make their parting as easy as possible by being upfront with his schedule. Apparently, Madison got the impression that he was simply enjoying his time before hitting the road again. She probably assumed he was the type of guy who never took relationships seriously.

He hated to admit it, but there was some truth to that. He hadn't been in a committed relationship in probably four to five years. He'd said himself that he lived a flighty life, hopping from one place to the next without digging in roots.

Did she feel like she was just another weekend fling? Another name to add to his list?

Eric didn't have a list.

He rarely dated when he was on a job. Sometimes he'd do some meaningless flirting, but he always made sure it never led to anything.

The screen of his laptop dimmed in front of him, about to time out due to his lack of activity. Sighing, he closed the device and leaned down to slide it into his bag.

No matter what she thought, his feelings for Madison were genuine. Maybe this was what he'd been waiting for, his sign that it was time to move on from this transient lifestyle. Time to settle down.

Feeling lighter than he had in a while, Eric stood as the intercom announced they were boarding his section. Things were going to work out, he just had to do what he could to let her know he really cared and then give it time.

*****

Madison stared at the dual screen monitors in front of her, the lines of text a faint blur to her unfocused gaze.

Everything was great. Life was great. She was great.

She nailed her dream job in her dream location. How could life get any better?

At least, that was what she kept telling herself.

Madison was missing Eric.

It was plain as day. But she was too proud to admit it. She'd gotten a few texts from him. Although, she just sent curt replies to whatever question he asked and left it at that. The one time he called, she'd let it go to voicemail.

It wasn't that she was trying to ignore him or even teach him a lesson. She, honestly, just wanted to protect herself.

She opened her heart the tiniest crack to him and had been regretting it ever since.

The worst part was that she'd known the type of guy Eric was. All the signs had been there. He was a guy looking for a non-committal, weekend fling. And Madison had willingly fallen right into his trap.

A faint buzz from her purse brought her out of her musings. She swiveled her chair so she could reach for her phone. Lighting up the screen, she saw a text from April.

Hey, want to come to my cycling class tonight? We can grab dinner after.

She smiled halfheartedly at her roommate's antics. This was a poorly veiled suggestion that they needed to have some girl chat. She knew April had noticed her moodiness over the last week. Madison had been dodging her questions about Eric every chance she got.

She leaned back in her chair, arching her spine to relieve the tension that had built up. She'd been typing this report for about an hour, and she could feel it.

It had been a while since she'd been to one of April's classes. Actually, it'd been a while since she'd done anything physical lately. Her bike ride when Eric had been in town had been over two weekends ago.

Why did everything always come back to Eric?

She sighed, the release of her breath just slightly therapeutic. Dodging her friend's questions wasn't helping the situation, as she well knew. Her thumbs shot back a reply.

Sure, as long as you promise to go easy on me. What time is the class at?

Seven. See you then.

Setting down her phone, she mentally blocked out the time that evening. Then she laughed to herself. It wasn't like she had anything else to fill her evenings these days. She would have no problem making time for it.

*****

"Hey, Dave, do you have a minute?"

Dave looked up from his monitor at her. "Madison, yes, of course I have time. Come in. What can I help you with?"

The upcoming service retreat had been on her mind all week. How would she and Eric interact with each other? How would she play a convincing girlfriend when she was still so mad at him?

Her mounting fears spurred her to make one last-ditch effort to get out of the trip.

Madison scratched at an imaginary itch on her arm. "Thanks, uh, well I-I wanted to ask again about the retreat. I'm just double checking that you actually have space for Ethan and me."

"Yes, you are definitely both accounted for." He smiled as he spoke, and with it, went any of her hope for escape.

He must have noticed her reaction, because his smile faltered slightly. "Will you guys have any problems making it? How is everything going with Ethan?"

The somewhat personal question surprised her. Or maybe it wasn't that personal; maybe she was just extra defensive, considering their whole relationship had been a sham. "Oh no, everything is great between us," she said brightly. "Just great. Ethan and I are both so excited. We can't wait!" Okay, maybe she laid the cheeriness on a little thick.

"Well, that's wonderful then." Despite his words, the question still hovered in his eyes. "We're scheduled to meet there Saturday morning at seven. Or I believe there's also a group carpooling from here if one of you needs a ride." He lifted his eyebrows.

She tried to swallow the lump in her throat. "Oh, we'll be fine. Ethan and I will, of course, just ride up together." Inwardly, she couldn't help thinking what a long drive that was going to be.

Dave tapped his chin. "Better make sure to ask Jill for the details in case I'm forgetting anything."

Madison made a mental note to stop by her desk on the way out. "Okay, thank you," she said, turning to leave.

His voice stopped her. "I just want you to know you're doing a great job, Madison. I can tell you're fitting in wonderfully with the team and with everything we stand for."

She looked back, a mixture of warmth and trepidation spreading through her at his words. "Thank you, sir. I've enjoyed my time so far."

"Terrific. We'll see you tomorrow then."

She gave him a smile but knew that it didn't reach her eyes. What she wouldn't give to go back two weeks and stop Eric from agreeing to the retreat. Now, more than ever, she was convinced she needed to make sure their relationship was believable. All of Dave's belief in her would crumble if he found out she'd been lying this whole time.

She hurried from the office, knowing she'd be cutting it close to April's class. After two borderline red lights and a quick stop at the locker room to change, she stepped into the spin room just as April welcomed everyone.

She gave her roommate a subtle wave before choosing one of the few empty bikes on the back row. She was lucky there were any open spots. April was a favorite in the gym.

By the time class finished, sweat dripped from her forehead, and a happy spike of endorphins filled her. It had been exactly what she needed. An hour of pushing herself physically let her clear her head of its conflicting thoughts.

April came around and slung an arm around her waist when all the other students were gone.

"How was class for you?" she asked as she wiped her brow with a towel.

Madison never understood how April managed to teach four to five classes a day. Just one wiped her out. "Awesome. You worked me over as usual." She wiped the sweat beading on her eyebrows. "See? Here's the proof." She swiped her now wet hand across April's arm, causing her roommate to jump back.

"Ew! I already deal with enough sweaty bodies all day. I don't need any more."

Madison laughed and reached down for her water bottle.

April turned for the door, calling over her shoulder, "I'm hungry. You ready to eat?"

Nodding, Madison followed her out.

They decided to eat at the little Greek place next door. After a quick shower and change in the locker room, they were sitting down to gyro sandwiches the size of their heads.

"I'm staaaarving," April moaned as she dug into her food.

"Even if I wasn't, this smell is enough to make me hungry." Madison talked around the bite of chicken she'd already put in her mouth.

After a few minutes of eating and moaning about how delicious it was, April wiped her hands in a napkin. "All right, we need to talk."

"About what?" Madison hoped if she played dumb, they could avoid the whole thing.

April wasn't distracted, though. "We need to talk about you and my brother. And why you've been moping around the house like a lost puppy the last two weeks since he left."

Well, so much for avoiding the topic. "I don't know what you're talking about. I haven't been acting differently." Madison scooped a spoonful of the cucumber tomato salad into her mouth. The tang of the feta cheese and red onion was perfection. She tried to focus on it instead of the hard stare April was giving her. "Maybe I'm just a little tired since I started my new job."

"You're in denial."

"I am not."

"You haven't left the house other than for work in two weeks."

"Who are you, my babysitter? And sure I have. I went to the grocery store at least two times."

"My point exactly."

Madison stuck her nose in the air.

"Mads...we can go back and forth like this until I dig the truth out of you, or you can just talk to me. What's going on between you two? Do I need to call up Eric and lay into him? What did he do?" April's forehead wrinkled as her brows drew together.

Madison shook her head. "Nothing. Honestly, April, he didn't do anything."

April's face softened. "Then, what's wrong? Why are you so sad?" She studied Madison for a second. "Do you have feelings for him? Ones he doesn't reciprocate?"

Madison bit her lip, trying to focus on the napkin she had begun to shred in her lap. "No, of course not... Maybe. I don't know." She took a deep breath. "I really don't know, April. I may have started developing feelings for him. But I know I shouldn't have. I knew he was only going to be here for a week or two. I kept telling myself to stay away." She grabbed the napkin bits and threw them on the table. "But he was just so dang nice! And he kept asking me to hang out with him. No matter how hard I tried to stop myself, I couldn't help falling for him a little."

"So what happened?"

"He left," Madison said simply.

"Yeah, but he's coming back this weekend. Isn't that something?"

"He's only coming back because he promised to do this charity project. It has nothing to do with me. After this, he'll go back to work." Madison waved her hands about her. "And even if we tried to do things long distance, those never end up well. Distance just makes everyone less committed." The name Claire ran distinctively through her mind, but she pushed it from her thoughts. In a subdued tone, she said, "I don't want someone I call on the phone at the end of every night and chat with for ten minutes. I want someone who is physically here. Someone who is a warm body I can cuddle up next to and watch a movie with."

April listened to Madison in silence, but her downturned eyes said exactly what she felt. "I get it, Mads. I really do. Long-distance relationships do seem a pain. But are you sure this is what you want?" She waited a half second before adding, "Because you don't look very happy."

Madison groaned and covered her face with her hands. "I don't even know what I want anymore. I thought I was making the right choice by ignoring my feelings. But it sure doesn't feel like it lately."

April reached forward and rubbed her arm. "I might be slightly biased, considering Eric is my brother, but maybe you should give him a chance. I don't think he's quite as flaky as you're imagining him to be."

"You're probably right," Madison said into her palms. Slowly, she lifted her gaze to April's. "But what if you're not?"

One corner of April's mouth lifted. "I guess you're just going to have to decide if he's worth the risk."

*****

It was 2 AM, and Eric stared hard at the bright screens of three monitors. The blue light from each of them felt like they were penetrating his eyeballs.

Leaning back, he rubbed his face then took a sip from the energy drink resting on the table.

He loved his work, but sometimes the hours were a killer. Most companies found it easiest for him to update their systems when others weren't working with them. That usually meant he came into work around five in the afternoon and left around three or four in the morning.

It was his second week on this project, and things were moving quite smoothly. He typed in a few more commands then began a reboot of the whole program. He tapped his fingers on the desk as he waited for the system to respond, his mind wandering aimlessly.

One of the bad things about working alone at night was having a lot of time with his thoughts. Lately, those thoughts had been consumed with Madison.

The longer he was away from her, the more he realized how much he didn't want to lose her. Not only was she strikingly beautiful, but more importantly, he'd never felt so completely at ease and comfortable with anyone else.

The lights flickered near the cables, and the machines began humming as they restarted. Fingers crossed there were no bugs.

He sighed as his mind wandered back to Madison. He knew nothing would evolve between them if things continued how they were. She was still mad at him. Her responses to his texts and calls left no doubt about that.

Which was why he needed to make his feelings clear. He needed to let her know he wanted to go all in—even if that change included moving on from freelance work.

It was crazy—maybe even presumptuous. But she was worth it.

Which was why this weekend retreat would be his chance to make sure Madison knew exactly where he stood.

The screens in front of him lit up, reminding him he still had a job to do in the meantime. He stifled another yawn and took a long swig from his energy drink.

Who knew, a career change might even lead him to getting some better nights of sleep.

Chapter 11

Madison started her second loop around the airport terminals. Her clock read 5:25 AM, and for probably the twentieth time that morning, she questioned why she was doing this.

Eric had landed in the Denver airport sometime in the last fifteen minutes, and she was there to pick him up for the weekend charity retreat.

It wasn't necessarily dread that filled her mind, just a general uneasiness. They had parted on a sour note. Would this whole weekend be a series of awkward interactions?

What made it worse was that, in her boss and co-workers' minds, Eric was her loving boyfriend, happy to come to this charity event with her. Madison wasn't sure if she could play the part of the happy couple for a whole 48 hours.

Her phone buzzed with a text.

Sorry, I got stuck behind a group getting off the plane. I'm standing at pickup curb number four.

Madison checked the signs and saw she was just approaching number two, so he should be up ahead in around two hundred yards. She peered through the dim light, the fluorescents overhead putting weird shadows on everyone. He stood out the second her eyes hit him, though. Looking as good as ever, he had one bag casually slung over his shoulder and a small carry-on in his other hand.

Her palms turned clammy on the steering wheel. Pulling over, she eased to a stop in front of him.

He ducked and peered into her window, his familiar grin lighting up his face when he confirmed it was her. He reached out for the door handle, giving it a solid yank with no success.

"Oh, dang it," Madison said, turning to hit unlock on her door.

When the locks all clicked open, he tried again with success. "Not sure if you really want to let me in?" he asked as he tossed his bags into the back seat.

"Something like that," Madison replied, grateful for the darkness hiding her blush. She pulled back into the street as Eric fastened his seatbelt. After a moment of heavy silence, she asked, "So, um, how was the flight?"

"Pretty good. There's something about sleeping in the upright position that leaves you feeling so restful," Eric said with a straight face.

Madison bit back a smile. "I'm sure."

"How about yourself? I'm assuming you don't normally wake up at 5 AM every day?" He had leaned his head against the window, his gaze resting on her.

"Actually, it was 4:30, but who's counting?" She gave him a smirk. "I'm good, ready for a day of serving."

"So, do you have any details of what we're actually doing at this place?"

"Not really." She shrugged and relaxed her tense grip from the steering wheel. "From what I could gather, I believe we're putting together kits of some sort."

"Well, I'm sure it will help someone, whatever it is."

Silence fell over them again, and this time, Madison had no idea how to fill it. She wished she could be as calm and collected as Eric appeared to be. He adjusted his position so his body was fully stretched out, his head leaned back against the headrest, and his eyes half closed. Did he feel no tension about being back with her again?

She pursed her lips. It was just like a man. Here, she had spent the last two weeks pining over him, going back and forth about how she should react when she saw him again and whether pursuing a relationship was worth it. He probably hadn't given their future a second thought after the obligatory texts he'd sent her.

"What's wrong?" His deep voice made her jump a little.

"What? What do you mean?"

He turned his head without lifting it from the headrest. "You shook your head like you were mad about something. Or were you just shaking off a fly?"

"Oh, it was nothing. I...I'm just a little tired. I'm trying to shake off...the sleepiness." Madison wanted to roll her eyes at herself.

"You should try sleeping sitting up."

She snorted against her will. "You're such a dork, Eric."

He shifted in his seat, bringing himself to a more upright position. "So, how were the last two weeks at work? Is it still your dream job?"

"Things are actually great. I'm loving it. Even more than I thought, if it's possible," Madison answered, glad for the change of topic. "I'm sure everyone might not think so, but the projects we're working on are fascinating." She continued explaining some of the things she'd done the last week.

Eric watched her with interest, asking questions and staying engaged during her whole monologue.

When she finally stopped for breath, she glanced at him. "Sorry, probably more information than you were looking for."

"No, I'm excited for you. I know this is something you've been working for." He paused and tapped his fingers on the windowsill before adding, "Not everything works out how we hope it will."

Madison wanted nothing more than to dig into that, ask him exactly what he spoke about. But he didn't add any more, and she wasn't ready to pry. Instead, she turned the topic to him.

"So, how about you? How is this new gig turning out?"

"It's good, nothing exciting. Just another job."

"So, what are you doing for them?" Madison had absolutely no knowledge about computers, but she was intrigued about what his daily work looked like.

"They are a company I've worked for before. They've just updated some of the services and products they offer." Eric went on to explain further, using a whole lot of vocabulary that Madison didn't understand. She tried to appear as interested and engaged as he had, though.

"So, what does your schedule look like at this place? You said you were going to be working nights?"

Eric nodded, reaching an arm to rest behind her seat. He wasn't actually touching her, yet she instinctively felt his nearness. "Yep, I've got the graveyard shift. I go in around five in the afternoon and leave sometime around three or four in the morning." He shrugged. "Usually, the only jobs I get that have normal hours is when I'm doing a total rehaul of a company's system. They have to shut down the office for a couple days for me to work on it. When I'm just making adjustments like this, though, I almost always work when their other employees are off."

"I guess that's just the nature of the job?"

"You could say that."

The silence that fell over them now was a more companionable one—at least to Madison. She turned the radio to an easy-listening station, the volume on low. They had another forty-five minutes before they reached the address Jill had given her. No point in blowing all their conversational topics for the weekend at once.

When her GPS announced they had two more miles until they turned off, Eric piped up.

"Do you mind if we stop at a gas station so I can grab something to eat quick?"

Madison glanced at him in surprise. "You haven't eaten anything?" She realized how dumb her question was the second she said it. Of course he hadn't eaten anything. He'd just been on a red-eye flight the last three hours. "I mean, of course we can stop." She cocked an eyebrow. "But not at a gas station. There can't be anything worth eating at one of those."

Eric lifted one finger. "I beg to differ. I have had many meals at gas station stops. I can't say they were all the healthiest meals, but that was probably my own fault. Most of the big stops have a decent selection of stuff." He took in Madison's cocked eyebrow. "I'm serious! If you look hard enough, you can probably even find some fresh fruit and stuff."

"All right, I'll stop. But I want to see these healthy food options you're talking about. From my memory, the only food I've ever seen at a gas station is stale donuts and dried out hot dogs."

"Don't forget the Slurpees. Those are a gas station essential."

She rubbed her forehead with her fingers. "Eric, there is probably more sugar in one of those things than a normal person should eat in a week."

"Exactly. Why do you think they taste so good?"

He clearly wasn't seeing her point of view.

Two minutes later, she pulled off at an exit that advertised a large gas station and truck stop. As Madison parked the car, she turned to him. "All right, I want you to wow me with all these nutritional options."

He gave her a little grin. "Right this way, madame."

Surprise hit Madison when they stepped inside the building. It really did look like a mini grocery store.

Eric reached for her, at the last second grabbing her elbow instead of her hand. Madison wondered about that as he led her down the first aisle. Maybe he wasn't as comfortable as he played off?

"First, over here, you'll see your fruits and veggies," he said.

Madison gazed at the two-foot section of packaged baby carrots and pre-sliced apples. She noticed a handful of bananas as well. "Well, I can't say I'm overwhelmed, but you're right; there are a few fruits and vegetables."

"Then, follow me right over this way." Eric started down the aisle, and Madison grabbed a banana before following him. They walked past the beverages which took up about half the store. The variety of soda and energy drinks was a little ridiculous.

Eric stopped in front of a section of muffins. "Here, you'll find an assortment of baked goods to fill your nutritional needs." He waved his arms about with a flourish.

Madison folded her arms as best she could while holding the banana. "Eric, please tell me you know muffins aren't actually healthy."

His face fell slightly. "What are you talking about? They're totally good for you." He picked one up and turned it over to look at the nutritional information. "See right here? It says...well, let's see..." He peered at the label a second longer before shoving it at Madison. "Look, one gram of fiber. Boom. Plus, this one is a blueberry muffin, so there's some fruit in there, too."

Madison just smiled and shook her head. "This muffin has 40 grams of sugar in it. That's over your ideal intake for the *entire* day." She glanced back at the label. "It has over half of the fat you should eat in a day, and very little protein or anything else good for you." She handed him back the muffin. "I don't want to scar you, but most muffins are actually cupcakes in disguise."

Eric stared up at the ceiling. "That's it, I can no longer hang out with you. You are ruining some of the best things in my life."

She patted him lightly on the arm. "The good thing is, you've got your whole life ahead of you to start swapping Pop-Tarts and blueberry muffins out for fruit and whole-grain breads."

Eric let out a long sigh. "I'm not sure if I want a life without Pop-Tarts and muffins."

Madison grinned as he put the muffin back.

With an exaggerated slump to his shoulders, he turned back to her. "Well, how about you find me something suitably healthy to eat?"

*****

As per Madison's GPS, they pulled up to a large parking lot at almost exactly 7 AM. It looked to be some sort of camp site. Eric could see a row of small cabins lined up behind the main office building. He stuffed the wrapper from his whole-grain bagel into the now empty Greek yogurt Madison had picked out for him. He had to admit, he felt pretty good after eating that combo.

Madison turned off the car and sat still for a moment.

He looked at her. The warm sunlight just peeking over the horizon gave her usually pale skin an almost tan glow. "You ready to do this...girlfriend?" They hadn't discussed their pretend boyfriend-girlfriend status at all during the drive, but Madison seemed on edge, and he didn't want to bring up the subject until she did.

Her jaw clenched for a split second. "Yes, if you would please continue pretending to be my boyfriend, that would be great. I haven't told anyone otherwise."

He nodded, wanting to laugh at her stiff manner. "Well, we seemed to do a pretty good job at the dinner. Let's just reenact that, and we should be good."

"Sounds like a plan." She opened her car door and hopped out.

Eric didn't miss the clipped tone to her voice, and he wondered if their fake relationship would even last the weekend. He wasn't exactly sure what was bugging her, but something simmered under the surface.

When they stepped into the main office, they found they weren't the first to arrive. Madison smiled and said hi to the others he assumed were her co-workers. He made his way to the front desk.

The woman behind it looked up at him, and he didn't miss the intrigue that flashed in her eyes. "Hi," she said, "are you here with the charity group, as well?"

"Yes," Eric replied, doing his best to ignore her interest. He reached for Madison and pulled her toward them. "My girlfriend and I are both part of the group. It should be listed under Madison Hudson and…" He paused, trying to recall the name she'd given him.

"And Ethan Ward," Madison finished over his shoulder.

"Yes, thank you, honey."

The woman's face had lost some of its eagerness at the word "girlfriend," and when Madison piped up, she turned purely professional. "Yes, Mr. Ward, just give me a moment…" Her fingers clipped across the keyboard. "Okay…looks like I have you two situated in cabin C." She turned and began pulling two key cards out of a drawer behind her.

Eric must have misheard her. "There should actually be—"

"Wait, did you say one cabin for the both of us?"

He'd been cut off by a flustered-looking Madison.

She elbowed her way in front of him. "Because we aren't—that is—there has to be—"

Eric put his arm around her, gently rubbing her shoulder in what he hoped was a calming way. "What my girlfriend is trying to say is, we'd like two separate rooms if possible." He leaned down and whispered in a loud voice, "She snores."

"I do not!" Madison said, pulling back and slugging him. "If anything, *you're* the snorer, with the purring that came from the couch all week long."

"So, you were watching me sleep, were you?" he asked, wondering how closely she had been paying attention to him two weeks ago.

"Ugh." Madison rolled her eyes and turned back to the receptionist. The woman had luckily been ignoring them and typing away.

"So, I have vacancy in two of the shared rooms booked by your group," the woman finally said with lifted eyebrows. "Does that meet your needs?"

"Yes. That will be perfect."

Eric thought Madison's reply was overly adamant, but he kept his feelings to himself. The woman gave them their separate room keys and wished them a pleasant stay. Eric glanced at Madison, trying to keep back a teasing smile.

Apparently, he didn't do a very good job, because after visibly lifting her nose in the air, she turned and made her way over to the group by the door without a word.

"Madison," one of the women said, reaching forward to give her a side hug. "So glad you guys could make it. I know a few people had to back out last minute."

Eric watched as Madison interacted with the others. She was so comfortable, so confident. He loved that about her. As a matter of fact, the only time he'd ever seen her show any type of nerves had been around him. He wasn't sure if that was a good or bad thing.

"Have you met Ethan yet?" Eric heard his stage name and snapped out of his thoughts.

Madison motioned him forward. "Ethan, this is Crystal. She works in the HR department. And this is Jessie, who works in...accounting, right?"

"Yep, I'm the number cruncher." Jessie reached forward to shake Ethan's hand. "You must be the boyfriend I've heard about?"

"Yep, that's me." Eric wondered exactly who she'd heard about him from. Madison hopefully?

"Dave mentioned Madison was bringing her boyfriend along. Apparently, you made a good impression, because he seems to think you're top notch." The woman smiled with an open face.

"What can I say, I'm a likeable guy." Eric shoved his hands in his pockets, not necessarily loving being the center of attention, but grateful to know he'd already had a good reputation.

The women went back to chatting.

He decided to go get the luggage from the car while he had a moment. He motioned to Madison, and she nodded, tossing him the keys.

Just as he closed the trunk of Madison's car, an SUV pulled up alongside him. "Ethan," a familiar voice called out.

He turned to see Dave and Liz getting out of the car. "Dave, good to see you." He set down one of the suitcases and reached out for a handshake.

"Thanks so much for coming out. We really appreciate it." Dave looked around Eric. "Where's Madison?"

"She's inside, chatting with some others." Eric motioned toward the suitcases. "I'm just the workhorse of the relationship."

Dave slapped his shoulder with a laugh. "I feel you. I'm still playing that role."

Liz came around the car, smiling at Eric as well. "So good to see you, Ethan. Happy you could be here with us."

Eric couldn't help feeling at ease with these people. He followed along behind them back inside.

"There you are, Madison. Look who we found in the parking lot," Dave said, turning to Eric as he entered the lobby.

Eric's eyes found Madison as she spun to face her boss. "Dave, Liz." She looked over at Eric. "Yeah, Er-Ethan said he'd be the porter for the day." She smiled brightly, and only Eric knew she was trying to cover up her gaffe.

Dave lifted up the suitcases he carried. "Me too."

Liz squeezed her husband's elbow. "It's because you're so big and strong, dear," she said, winking at everyone else.

They all laughed, and Dave and Liz went to check in. Eric took his place by Madison.

When everyone's conversations resumed, he leaned down and whispered in her ear, "Good catch. Maybe you should just tell everyone your nickname for me is Eric?"

She didn't say anything, although he saw her lips twitch slightly.

Over the next fifteen minutes, the group got big enough to fill the lobby. They agreed to give everyone a half hour to get settled in their rooms before meeting in the front again.

A concourse of shuffling and people gathering their stuff started. Eric grabbed both of their suitcases and followed Madison out the door.

"Here, I can take that," she said, reaching for her bag.

He held it out of her grasp. "I got it. I'll just drop it off for you." Sometimes her independent nature made being a gentleman difficult.

Madison's room was one of the first cabins. The door was already open when they got there, so Madison poked her head in hesitantly. "Hello?" she said. Eric stood a few feet off.

A second later, Jessie walked out. "Madison, are you my roommate?" Her broad smile filled her face.

"Looks like it," Madison said with an equally pleased look. She turned and motioned to him, "Here, you can just put that right inside the door."

He stepped forward with her suitcase, setting it down where she indicated. The room had a nice but simple layout—two queen-size beds covered with patchwork quilts, and a small, rustic desk and lounge chair to the left.

"Looks homey," he said as he straightened. "You sure you'll be okay here without me? You won't get cold tonight or anything, right?" He loved messing with her. There was something about the immediate flush that rose up her cheeks when she got flustered.

"Yes, Ethan. I'll be perfectly fine without you, *as usual*." Her gritted teeth gave him all the hint he needed.

"Well, I'll go check out my room. See you in about twenty." He stepped off the porch, whistling a random tune.

Despite his carefree appearance, his mind churned inside. Would sharing a room with him have been that terrible to Madison? She seemed a little too relieved to be in her own place. He wasn't sure of the answer, and he wasn't sure he wanted to know it.

*****

Madison shuffled her feet as she stood next to Jessie and a few others in front of the main building. She tried to keep her eyes on the ground instead of scanning the cabins. She was fine without Eric; she didn't need him by her side every minute during this trip. But she couldn't stop her traitorous eyes from glancing up every few seconds.

When she saw him emerge from the cabin two away from her own, she straightened and turned to Jessie, pretending to be engrossed in the conversation. She soon felt a hand lightly brush around her waist and pull her in for a squeeze.

"Hey, hon, did you miss me?" His voice was low but definitely loud enough for anyone around her to hear.

She bit back her quick retort and, instead, gave him a strained smile. "Yes, always." She didn't know why she felt so snappy when he gave her his little terms of endearment. He was simply playing the part she asked him to. It was probably just the knowledge that it was all fake.

She tried to shake off the bad vibes and pay attention to the current situation. Dave had gathered people over by a tree, and so she nodded Eric in that direction. "Looks like we're going over there."

He didn't say anything, just followed her.

Liz was, apparently, the one really in charge of this event as she began handing out tasks and dividing them into groups. She naturally put Eric and Madison together, giving them the assignment of organizing toothbrushes, toothpaste, and dental floss.

They were directed to the rec room with two or three other groups.

Madison decided to take a very businesslike approach to the day. They were there to serve the needy, after all. No one would expect her and Eric to be cozying up to each other. "All right, Liz said the toothbrushes and toothpaste should be together," Madison said as they stepped inside the large room. The vaulted ceiling gave the space a cool, airy feel despite the warmth of the morning. "The floss supposedly got boxed up near the soap and shampoo, though." She glanced at Eric. "You want to gather up the toothbrushes and toothpaste while I look for the floss?"

Eric simply gave her a thumbs up and turned to sort through boxes.

She let out the breath of air she'd been holding. Good, he must have been on the same page with her in terms of their interaction for the day.

Madison eventually found the floss and carried them to where Eric had begun placing the toothpaste and toothbrushes.

As she brought over the last of her boxes, Eric took out a set of keys and ripped open one of his. Inside, were perfect rows of individually wrapped toothbrushes.

"Well, looks like these were labeled correctly," Eric said. He proceeded to rip open all the others.

Madison tried not to watch the muscles in his forearms moving with each stroke. Somehow, despite his apparent love for junk food, Eric managed to stay in decent shape. When he'd picked up her suitcase earlier, he'd swung it around like it weighed as much as a feather—something Madison knew to be untrue, due to the fact that she'd packed enough clothes for a two-week trip. (Simply because she wasn't sure of the work they were doing. It had absolutely nothing to do with the fact that Eric would be there.) She wondered what he'd look like with his shirt off...

"All right, how do you want to work this?" Eric asked. He held up a handful of toothbrushes. "How about I add the toothbrush and toothpaste to the bags, then you add the floss and tie them closed?"

Madison nodded. "Sounds good." She started shoving boxes around until they were in a line.

"All right, so we need one toothpaste." Eric dropped one of the small tubes into a plastic bag. "And one toothbrush." He added a plastic brush before handing the bag off to Madison. She took the bag as he started another. "One toothpaste...and one toothbrush," he said again, passing the second bag off.

"You know," Madison said, trying not to snort after his third recitation of toothpaste and toothbrush, "this would probably go a little faster if you didn't describe every step."

"I'm taking the systematic approach," Eric said with a grin as he finished off a fourth bag. This time, as he passed it, their fingers touched, the momentary contact freezing Madison in place. Instead of moving on like nothing happened, Eric enhanced the moment by trailing his fingers along her hand, a slight upturn to his lips.

That look stirred her into motion, quickly pulling the bag and her arm back. He was messing with her again, and she didn't like it. Here she was, trying to suppress these dumb feelings, and he just wanted to see how often he could bring them to the surface.

Clearing her throat loudly, she spent the next few minutes trying to appear completely composed and nonchalant about the whole thing. If Eric thought he could push her buttons with a little hand touching, he was definitely wrong. She'd show him.

The slight tension between them only broke when Liz came by with more bags. "How are things going?" she asked, looking over their progress. "Whoa, you guys are fast."

Madison looked at the pile of completed bags they'd packed. They *were* moving right along. Apparently, tension increased efficiency.

"Mads and I make a good team," Eric said with a warm look at her.

She had a hard time remembering her anger when those blue eyes looked at her like that.

"Obviously," Liz responded candidly. She made a flitting motion with her fingers. "Well, don't let me interrupt you. Keep at it." She hurried off to check on the other groups.

"So, how do you think everyone is taking our status as boyfriend and girlfriend?" Eric asked, his voice low.

Madison eyed him. "Well, with acting skills like yours, how could they doubt us?"

"Acting skills?"

Madison almost called him out right then. Called him out for messing with her emotions. For being the careless playboy he obviously was. But there were too many people in the room, and she didn't want to create a scene.

Instead, in a quiet voice, she added, "You do a great job of playing the affectionate suitor. No one could doubt your performance."

Considering the way his hands froze, her comment must've hit home. But she didn't want an open discussion right then. She wasn't emotionally ready for it, nor was this the right place. She quickly turned back to the packing and willed him to do the same.

He apparently got the hint, because a minute later, he quietly began filling more bags with toothpaste and toothbrushes.

They worked from then on in complete silence. Mysteriously, there were no more accidental hand brushes or contact between them. Eric must have realized she was not in the mood for games.

An hour later, they had five boxes filled to the brim with tooth care products.

"So," Eric said, running a hand through his hair, "do you know where we need to put these?"

"No." Madison grabbed the remaining bags they hadn't used. "I'll go find Liz and see what she wants us to do next."

She found Liz outside on the open pavilion. There were two other groups of people packing things alongside her and Dave.

"Hey, Liz," Madison said, coming up from behind her. "Ethan and I finished our load. What should we do with all the bagged items?"

"Awesome," Liz said. "Why don't you bring them outside? There's more room to assemble the final boxes here than there is inside the rec room."

Madison was about to turn when Dave piped up. "How are you guys already finished?"

She just smiled. "I guess we just make a good team." She thought about that comment as she made her way back to Eric. They did make a good team. In more ways than one. But was she the only one that thought so?

She reached the room and found Eric leaning against the wall, typing something on his phone. "You texting your girlfriend?" She bit her lip after the juvenile comment came out.

He wiggled his eyebrows. "Wouldn't you like to know?" Pocketing his phone, he continued. "No, just answering a billing question from my assistant, Claire."

The name sent alarms through Madison's head. "Claire?"

Eric glanced at her. "Yeah, she's my virtual assistant. She takes care of all the scheduling and other miscellaneous things I hate doing." He squinted his eyes for a second. "I think she's been working for me for about three years now." He shrugged. "She's a sweet lady who lives down in Arizona, actually. She treats me more like a son than her boss."

Madison clenched her teeth into a smile, but inside, her thoughts were reeling. The Claire she'd based half of her fears on was his virtual assistant? A woman who treated him like a *son*? How old was she?

"So, what did Liz say?"

"Uh…" Madison tried to focus on the present. "They want us to bring the kits outside. We'll assemble everything together out there."

He stood up and pocketed his phone. "All right." Hefting one of the boxes on his shoulder, he headed out.

Madison followed suit, grabbing one of the smaller ones.

By the time they got all their bags out there, Dave had begun gathering people for a lunch break. Everyone made quick work of distributing the food catered in from a local sandwich shop and finding places on the grass to sit and eat.

Madison settled in a spot in the shade, easing herself into a cross-legged position on the grass. Eric relaxed next to her, close but not quite touching.

Eventually, Jessie and Crystal came and sat next to them. "So, what are you two packing?" Jessie asked as she began peeling an orange.

"We are doing a bunch of dental items. Toothbrushes, toothpaste, etc," Madison answered. "How about you two?"

"We've got deodorant and facial wipes," Crystal said. "You never realize how much you take for granted simple things like deodorant."

They all nodded, and a lighthearted discussion ensued about products they couldn't live without. Madison tried to focus but couldn't get her mind away from the new insight she had about the mysterious Claire. She bit her lip, sheepishly thinking she might have overreacted.

She watched Eric out of the corner of her eye, noticing how easily he integrated himself into the conversation. Similar to the charity dinner, he seemed to fit right in with no problem.

She fiddled with the cap on her water bottle. Instead of dancing around the issue, she needed to come straight out and ask him where his feelings lay. No more guessing. Was she just some weekend fling? Or something more?

Now, the only problem was deliberating what exactly to say.

Chapter 12

Eric didn't know what had happened over the last two weeks, but whatever it was, it hadn't been good. Not that he expected Madison to welcome him with open arms. But her indifferent attitude was worse than he'd thought.

He glanced over at her as she added another bag to the kit. She'd been pretty quiet ever since lunch. Her wispy hair fell over her face as she bent for another bag, and she brushed it back impatiently.

Eric's hand itched to reach out and comb through her strands himself. He wondered if they were as silky smooth as they looked right now. He was sure he'd touched them before, likely during that kiss they'd shared in the arcade parking lot, but he'd probably been far too distracted by the feel of her lips to notice her hair in his hands.

Her natural beauty struck him once again. Here she was, jeans and a T-shirt, probably no makeup on or anything, and he couldn't keep his eyes off of her.

Looking at his hands, he realized he'd been holding the same bag for a minute now. He rubbed his eyes and got back to work.

That was it. Enough dancing around the subject. After dinner, he would get her alone to talk. To see exactly where they stood.

"Alright, everyone," Dave's loud voice cut into Eric's thoughts. The way Madison jumped made him think she'd been lost in hers as well. "We're going to call it good for the day. We still have a solid twelve hours tomorrow to finish the job." Dave grinned broadly. "We're having pizza in the rec room; feel free to head on over."

"Ugh, my back. I need to bring a chair tomorrow. I'm too old to be hunched over like this," Jessie said, rubbing the small of her back as they walked.

"Haha, I should bring one myself," Madison said. "For not moving much today, I sure am tired."

Eric instinctively reached out to massage her shoulders, although her muscles seemed to tense up even more at his touch.

After a slight falter in her step, she said, "I'm really fine. You don't need to do that."

"I want to," he said, giving her a wink. "I can't let my girlfriend end the day with a sore neck."

"Oh, well, um, thank you," she said, an uncertain smile on her lips as her eyes darted to the others around them.

Nobody was really paying them much attention, but Eric could see her insecurity, so he slowly let his hands drop. "I'll finish your massage after dinner if its still hurting," he said, giving her shoulders one more squeeze.

Inside the rec room, a row of extra-large pizzas were laid out along with breadsticks and soda. Eric followed along behind Madison, each filling their plates with cheesy goodness.

"Are you sure this is a Sube-Nutritionals-approved meal?" he whispered in her ear. A sense of satisfaction ran through him when goosebumps broke out along her neck. Maybe she did feel something for him, after all.

She swallowed but quickly smiled at him. "I'm pretty sure I saw a green pepper on one of the pizzas, so we're good."

"Alright, you're the nutritionist here." It was his turn to swallow. Every time she turned that wide grin on him, a jolt of adrenaline pumped through his veins. "Hey, so you want to go eat alone for a bit? I saw some picnic tables over by my cabin."

Madison nodded, although he noticed she was biting her lip. "Sure, um, let me just grab a drink."

They made their way outside, this time Madison following Eric, her eyes sedately pinned on the food in her hands. He headed toward the picnic table he'd mentioned.

"Nothing but the best for you, ma'am," he said, pulling out a metal chair with a flourish.

"I've always loved a good picnic table," she responded dryly as she set her plate down.

He settled his chair right next to her and tried to focus on the food on his plate and not the way her shoulders seemed to stiffen at his nearness. Were her nerves a good sign or a bad one? Despite the thick layer of cheese and still-steaming sausage, he wasn't enjoying a single bite. He needed to use this time to connect with Madison, but the pressure was getting to him.

"So, you said you're enjoying working at Sube. Do you think this is a long-term job for you?" Maybe if he could get her talking about careers, he could slide in his plan to settle in Denver. A plan that she was essential to.

Madison stared off into the distance as she chewed. "I don't know, to be honest," she eventually answered. "Sometimes, I think this could be a lifelong company. Why would I move? But at the same time, I can see myself itching for something new in a few years."

Eric nodded, knowing exactly what she meant. "I get it. That's part of the drive that got me to start freelancing. There's something exciting about doing new things every so often." He pulled an olive off the slice in his hands. "What do you think you'll do if you get married?" He wasn't sure why he asked the question. It came out before he really had time to think.

Madison choked on her water. "Ma-married?"

"Yeah, well, I'm assuming one day you'll get married and have kids." Eric wiped his hands on a napkin and leaned back. He started this vein of conversation; he might as well continue it. "Will you keep working then?"

"Gosh, I don't know. I mean, probably. At least until I have kids or something. I really haven't thought about it much." She put down her water bottle, fiddling with the screw-top lid.

"Ah, come on, a girl like you? It'll probably happen sooner than you think." Eric tried to keep things playful, but he couldn't remove the serious note to his tone.

Madison's cheeks pinked, and those blue eyes of hers darted back and forth. "Well, considering I had to ask my roommate's brother to be my pretend boyfriend for the weekend, it's probably not on the immediate horizon." She cleared her voice, and her fingers began tapping the table almost of their own accord.

Her obvious discomfort had him reaching for her hand, wishing he could give her a glimpse of how he saw her. "Ah, c'mon, Mads." He paused, waiting for her to pull back. When she didn't, he continued. "You act like there's nothing between us."

There, he'd laid it out on the table. Dropped the bait for her to pick up.

She stared down at their hands then up at him. "What exactly is there between us?"

He noticed her fingers shook slightly. Tightening his hold, he turned toward her. "What about two weeks ago? You can't tell me there wasn't some connection there." He hoped that by coming straight out and talking about it, they could get to the core of whatever issue Madison was having. Because as cocky as it sounded, Eric was pretty sure his feelings weren't one-sided.

She said nothing, just stared at the plate in front of her. "Eric…" Her words trailed off. She swallowed and started again. "Last week was fun…but we both—"

"Hey, Madison, you done? I'm headed over to our cabin now."

They both turned at Jessie's interruption. She waved at them from about ten yards away.

"Oh, okay…yeah, wait for me. I'll be right there," Madison responded.

Eric rubbed a hand over his eyes, regretting agreeing to separate cabins. He'd never get alone time with Madison at this rate.

Madison stood and glanced at him. "Maybe we can talk about this more tomorrow?" she asked as she picked up her paper plate.

"Sure." She didn't seem to have any intention of saying a formal goodbye, but he knew it would look weird if they didn't do something. They were supposed to be dating, after all. "I hope you sleep well tonight; we have a long day tomorrow," he said as he stood.

She watched his movements cautiously, eyes widening as he stepped closer.

Without waiting to gauge her reaction, he wrapped his arm around her waist, lifting her up to her toes as he brought her mouth to his.

Despite her dismissal that there was anything between them, her kiss said otherwise.

He started slowly at first, his lips barely brushing hers. But when her hands encircled his neck, pinning him to her, he stopped holding back.

He could feel the pulse of her heart beating rapidly against him. Or was that his?

Finally remembering they had an audience, he managed to pull back, everything in his body screaming at him to keep going. With his breath coming short, he slowly lowered her to the ground.

Madison covered her mouth with a hand, shock in her eyes. She recovered quickly, though. Uttering a simple "goodnight," she turned to join Jessie who had tactfully been studying the grass.

Eric watched her go, waiting until she was out of sight before sitting down again with a thud. He scrubbed a hand down his face. His lips still tingled from their kiss, and there was an undeniable ache to have her back in his arms. No matter what she said, her response to his kiss showed she felt something too.

A steely determination straightened his spine—he no longer wanted to be the fake boyfriend. He wanted it all. He wanted Madison.

*****

At breakfast the next morning, Madison sat alone, scribbling furiously in her notebook. It was one of those planners that contained just about everything in her life. Her calendar, shopping list, to-do items. Lately, it had even become a journal of sorts, a way to process her feelings. And her feelings about Eric definitely needed some processing.

Her pen flew across the paper, writing down every pro and con, every good and bad feeling about him. She had to admit, the positives outweighed the negatives.

"You saving this place for anyone?"

Eric's deep voice made Madison literally jump out of her chair. "Oh my gosh, you scared me!" She had purposely woken up extra early, assuming she'd have a solid half an hour to herself. Well, maybe not purposely. More like she couldn't sleep and had finally given up on the impossible task.

"Apparently." Eric held a plate filled with scrambled eggs and toast. He didn't sit, just stood, staring down at her. Madison realized he was waiting for an answer.

She shoved aside her still unopened yogurt cup and plate of toast and motioned for him to sit. Seamlessly, she closed her notebook and slid it into her bag, hoping he hadn't noticed it.

"What were you writing?" he asked as he sat.

So much for not noticing.

"It's…ah...just my to-do list. You know, gotta keep on top of things." She laughed nervously.

Eric quirked a brow but moved past it. "You not hungry today?" He nodded toward her uneaten food as he took a giant bite of his heavily buttered toast.

"Not really." Madison grabbed her yogurt and started peeling it open anyway. "I guess I better eat something, though."

"Are you feeling sick?" Eric pressed, his brow furrowed.

"No, I'm really fine." Madison took a bite of yogurt as if to prove she told the truth. "So, what do you think we're going to be doing today?" she asked, deliberately trying to change the subject.

Eric eyed her but dropped it. "Well, I know we have to finish up a few more of those boxes from yesterday. I heard Dave talking about packing food, though, so I wouldn't be surprised if we're doing something along those lines." He smiled, his normally hollow cheeks filling out with the expression.

Madison brushed back a stray hair, suddenly wishing she had spent more time doing her makeup this morning. She'd simply pulled her hair back into a loose ponytail and thrown on her favorite jeans and a basic white shirt. Why hadn't she put on something a little more flattering? Maybe her blue sundress with the fitted waistline?

As she eyed Eric, though, she almost laughed.

He was such a guy. Still sporting bed hair, he wore shorts and a wrinkled T-shirt. She guaranteed he hadn't worried about his appearance once this morning. Although, despite it, he did look pretty good. His lack of effort gave him a manly, disheveled look that forced her to take a quick sip of her ice water to cool off.

They chatted a little more about the events of the day as others trickled in in various stages of sleepiness.

"Hey, can everybody bring it in in about five minutes?" Dave's voice finally echoed from one corner of the rec room. Eric shoved the last bite of toast in his mouth, and Madison did the same with her yogurt.

As they stood, Eric reached for her plate. "Here, let me take that for you."

"Thank you," she said, offering him a smile. "You're such a gentleman."

"My mama raised me right."

His joking made her feel more lighthearted than she had in days. She liked this better. This was the easy companionship they had had that first week together. The awkwardness of the last twenty-four hours left her constantly unsettled and nervous.

A few minutes later, Dave began his pep talk for the day. "Yesterday was awesome. We accomplished so much together. So, let's make sure we bring that same energy today, because this is our last chance to make a difference." After a cheer from the group, Liz started calling out everyone's assignments for the morning. As Eric had guessed, they were packing food. He and Madison were grouped with another couple, putting together snack bags of granola bars, crackers, and beef jerky.

Twenty minutes later, they were in the groove and working as a seamless team. The other couple was a little older, probably somewhere in their late forties. The man worked in the sales department of Sube Internationals, so Madison hadn't interacted with him yet.

"So, which one of you works at Sube?" the man's wife, Jenny, asked.

Eric nodded at Madison. "She's the smart one. I'm just here for my muscles."

Madison just shook her head as the woman laughed goodnaturedly. "So, what do you do then?"

"I work in computer technology."

"Well, that sounds like you need a little bit of intelligence for that." Jenny grabbed a new box of granola bars and began tearing it open. "I'm assuming you work somewhere in Denver, too?"

Eric glanced at Madison before responding this time. She wondered how he would explain his work to the woman. Would he downplay his traveling to make them seem like a more settled couple? She sent him an encouraging smile.

"Well, I'm actually a freelance technician. So, my work location can vary from project to project." He lifted a box of cheese crackers on the table and began divvying them out.

Madison reached over for a pile of the bagged snacks and added them to her kits.

"So, you must travel a lot. How does that work between you two?" Jenny continued.

This woman was either really bored or loved hearing about other's lives, Madison thought to herself, glad Eric was getting the brunt of the questions.

Eric had no problem with the interrogation, though. "That's really the worst part about it. All the traveling means I don't get to spend nearly as much time with Madison as I'd like." As he spoke, he unexpectedly pulled her into a side hug and kissed the top of her head.

Dang, he was good at this boyfriend stuff, Madison thought, knowing her cheeks were reddening slightly. She couldn't deny enjoying the moment, though, as she melted into him. She *had* determined to let things take their course between them, right?

Jenny nodded. "I understand exactly." She pointed at her husband who was digging through a box of beef jerky. "Tom, here, traveled nonstop the first few years of our marriage. I finally had to put my foot down and tell him he either needed to travel less or change jobs." She shrugged. "It was just too much for our family. I couldn't do everything alone, and Tom was missing too much of our lives."

Eric nodded, no joking in his face now.

For some reason, Madison felt the need to jump in and defend her fake boyfriend. "Ethan is extremely good at what he does. Sometimes, it's just hard to give up all the great opportunities that pop up for him. But we're working it out." Eric's eyes had narrowed at her, but she simply turned back to the crackers she was supposed to be organizing.

"You'll be fine," Jenny said with a knowing look. "If you're really committed to each other, things always work out."

Her simple statement hit Madison like a rock. Was that all it took? Did they just need to decide whether or not they were really committed to each other and go from there?

The conversation switched to more lighthearted subjects. Jenny and her husband were fun companions, but the same question never stopped running through Madison's head.

By noon, they broke for another catered brown-bag lunch.

She and Eric grabbed their food and went over to the metal table that had, apparently, become their spot. It was far enough from the group that they felt like they had a measure of privacy without being too removed.

"This is probably the best ham-and-cheese sandwich I've ever had," Eric said, leaning back in his chair with his sub in one hand.

"That probably just means you're about as hungry as I am," Madison responded, lifting up her turkey sandwich in a mock toast.

"It's possible. Who knew putting together boxes of food could make you so hungry?" Eric took a swig from his water bottle.

"So, are you going to volunteer at charity events more often now?" she asked, digging through her brown bag.

He nodded. "Probably. It feels good to know I'm helping others instead of just focusing on myself." He eyed her. "How about you?"

She looked up and nodded. "Yeah, I hope so. Sometimes it's easy to get so caught up in my life that I forget how blessed I really am." She fished out the bag of pretzels she'd been looking for. Grasping both sides of the bag, she pulled. It didn't seem to want to open, though.

"Here, you want me to get that for you?" Eric asked, extending his hand.

Madison rolled her eyes. "I think I can open my own pretzels." She grabbed both sides of the bag again and gave a solid yank. The seam slipped open easily this time, catching Madison by surprise. Her elbow, unfortunately, went wide, knocking both Eric's water and her purse off the table.

The contents inside the pretzel bag flew through the air, and Eric's open bottle hit the table with a splat, managing to drench her shirt before bouncing on the ground.

"Oh gosh, what did I just do?" Madison cried, jumping up.

"I told you you should've let…" Eric's words trailed off, and she looked up to see him quickly glancing away, cheeks flamed red. She peered down at herself and realized she was wearing a white T-shirt. One that the water had essentially made see-through.

"Uh, I think I'm gonna go change real quick," she stuttered, folding her arms in front of her.

Eric looked down, but not before she saw a smile stretch across his face. "I don't know, you look pretty good in a wet shirt."

"Oh, you dork." She slugged his shoulder and hurried away. She called back over her shoulder, "Don't eat all my food. I'll be back in a minute."

*****

Eric smiled, thinking about the blush that filled Madison's cheeks at his comment. He was obviously not serious, but it was fun messing with her.

He gathered up the items that spilled out of her purse. It wasn't an overly filled bag. He knew some women liked to carry the world inside their purse, but Madison's was fairly simple with just a wallet, her phone and keys, some sort of lipstick, and the calendar she'd been writing in earlier. He had tried to not let his interest show, but he'd been very intrigued by it that morning. She seemed so defensive and secretive about it.

The planner had fallen facedown on the ground, the pages open to somewhere in the middle.

He bent down to pick it up, flipping it over to look at the page it opened to. What he saw made him freeze. There, titled in the margin in bold letters, read: Excuses for Breaking Up with Eric.

Below it, listed out various ideas. Things such as: *he moved, we got in a big fight, he cheated on me.*

He scanned the page, not sure what it was at first. Then, understanding hit him. These were the excuses she would give people when they went back to real life. The life where they weren't actually dating. He remembered her saying she was worried about explaining their breakup to others. He'd thought it was a strange concern at first. However, now that he knew Madison better, he knew that she took care of things down to the minute detail.

He closed the notebook and shoved it in her purse. So, this was what she had been writing that morning. Here he was, about to explain that he wanted to move back to

Colorado to be near her, and she was just concerned with how to explain his absence to everyone at work.

Obviously, she was a better actress than he'd given her credit for. That kiss last night had all been for their audience.

He shoved his plate aside, disgusted with himself and how easily he'd been played. What was his problem? Obviously, she wanted nothing more than a temporary boyfriend. Hadn't she said that enough times? Hadn't every interaction he'd had with her this trip been evidence of that?

Well, he wouldn't burden her with his pursuits anymore. He'd be on a plane for Boston tonight, and then everything would be back as it was before. For good.

What he really wanted to do was get out of there right now. He didn't know if he could spend another six hours pretending to be the happily in love boyfriend. He should act like a jerk the rest of the day and give Madison some extra fuel for one of her breakup scenarios.

Eric grabbed a napkin and mopped up the spilled water on the table, no longer interested in his food.

He looked over toward Madison's cabin and was rewarded by the sight of her hurrying back, a dry, form-fitting black shirt replacing her wet, white one. Man, she looked good. His stomach clenched, knowing her indifference to him, and he dropped his gaze. He had to stick to his resolve. There was no future for him and Madison, and he wasn't going to hope for one.

"Sorry again about that," Madison said as she walked up to the table. She glanced down at her purse fully restored.

"Thanks for picking up all my stuff, too. I promise, I'm not usually this klutzy."

Instead of giving her a teasing response, Eric simply nodded. "No worries. I'm going to go grab something in my room. I'll be back in time to start working again."

He ignored Madison's confused expression and the twinge in his chest as he turned to leave. Good, he was glad he wasn't the only one who felt lost.

Chapter 13

Madison wasn't sure what had happened at lunch, but something had changed in Eric. He wasn't necessarily mean or rude; he was just totally distant the rest of the day. He worked alongside everyone the same as before. However, every hint of his usual charm was gone. Where were the joking comments and the teasing looks?

She honestly couldn't fathom what it had been. But whatever had been warming up between them had now turned cold.

"Is your box empty down there?" Madison asked, indicating to the granola bars at his feet.

He held up the cardboard container, not looking at her. "Yep, all gone."

"All right, we're out of the crackers, too." It was just them left since Jenny and Tom had had to leave early that afternoon. One of their kids had a recital they needed to get back for. Madison glanced at the clock—just after five. Dave was providing dinner for everyone, so she assumed they'd leave right after that.

"Do you have all your stuff packed up? We might as well put our suitcases in the car now."

Eric nodded. "You know me, I pack light. Why don't you put yours outside your door, and I'll grab it on my way to the car."

Madison bit her lip, wishing she had something else to say, something to cut through his businesslike manner. Nothing came to mind. "Alright, I guess I'll meet you in the rec room for dinner."

Eric nodded, his eyes averted as he hurried to his cabin.

Madison headed for hers as well, dragging her feet slightly. She had felt so good before lunch. The decision to try and turn things around with Eric had brought a light to her mind that had been turned off with his attitude change.

She sighed and opened the door to her room. Her stuff was already packed up; she just had to get a few toiletries from the bathroom. That finished, she set the suitcase at the bottom of the steps, no sign of Eric yet.

She made her way to the rec room alone, deciding she might as well put a good face on for the last minutes they were here.

Dave stood just inside the door, his happy demeanor proving the weekend had been a success for him. "Madison, come eat," he said as she walked in. "Where's Ethan?"

"He'll be along in a minute. He was putting the suitcases in the car."

"Good man," Dave said with a wink. "You better go get a plateful before it's all gone. So far, I think the steak is my favorite, just for a heads up."

Dinner was tacos. A wide assortment of different meats, as well as all the toppings she could imagine, filled the table. She filled up her plate, all the while keeping her eye on the door.

When Eric finally entered, he went straight to the line and made himself a large plate of food, not stopping to talk to anyone. He didn't even look for her. Instead, he just plopped down in the first empty seat available.

Madison turned from the chair she'd been saving for him, trying to ignore the way her heart hitched tightly. *How could such a simple action say so much*, she thought as she sank further into her own seat.

She wasn't hungry anymore, but she robotically ate a few bites. The rest she simply tossed in the trash. After making the rounds and saying goodbye to the few people left, she walked up to Eric, still sitting in his isolated chair.

"Ready to go?" Her emotionless tone matched his expression.

"Yep," he said as he tossed his paper plate in the nearby trash.

Five minutes later, they were sitting in her car, starting one of the longest and quietest drives she had ever taken.

*****

Madison walked in the door of her apartment late that evening and lasted about three seconds before bursting into tears.

April jumped up from the couch where she was watching a *Friends* rerun for probably the 100th time.

Without saying anything, she wrapped Madison up in a hug, then led her crumbling roommate to the couch.

"Honey, what happened?" April asked, her eyes searching Madison's. "You were supposed to come back from the weekend having figured out that you two are the perfect couple!"

"I don't know," Madison said, finding a small measure of comfort from the familiar burst of lavender that came from the couch. "I don't know what happened. I started out so determined to just get through the weekend. Get through two days of making everyone believe Eric and I were in a committed relationship."

She stared at the coffee table, picking up a few stray kernels from April's bowl of popcorn and crumbling them in her hand.

"But…" April prompted.

"But then…I don't know. Things changed. He was so fun and nice, just like before. I realized I was being dumb and juvenile and maybe I should give things another try with him." She chucked a popcorn kernel into the bowl, an echoing ting as it bounced off the edges. "Then, the second I decided to give it a try, your brother flipped a switch and froze me out. He was like a totally different person. I don't know what changed!"

April cocked her head. "You have no idea what set him off? I mean, Eric's not perfect by any means,"—her roommate waved her hands about—"but it seems like something must've happened to make him act so weird."

Madison shrugged. What she wouldn't give to just erase the last two days. "I have no idea. All I know is I'm hopeless when it comes to men, and I'm going to die an old hag with only my ten cats to mourn me."

"All right, rein in the drama, honey," April said, propping her feet up on the table. "So, how are we going to figure this out? I think the key is just to get some clarity about what's bothering Eric. Did you ask him?"

"No. What was I supposed to say? 'Hey, Eric, how come you're no longer flirting and teasing me all the time? Don't you like me anymore?'" She puffed out her lips in a pout.

"Well, at least we would've known what he was thinking."

Madison rolled her eyes at April's practical tone. "Besides, I don't think I even care to know what's bothering him. Maybe it's better this way." She began to twirl her hair. "It would definitely be a whole lot simpler, that's for sure."

"Simpler doesn't necessarily mean happier, Mads." Her friend leveled her with a look.

Madison knew April was right. She could try her best to put Eric and the last two weeks totally behind her, but she didn't think that would make her feel any better. She rested her head on the back of the suede couch.

"You need to really evaluate what you want in life and what brings you happiness," April continued. "Because from what I could see, being with Eric made you happy. As soon as he left, you turned all weepy and mopey, like the sun had stopped shining."

Madison narrowed her eyes. "I did not."

April took a long, deep breath. "Look, I'm not here to debate whether or not you emotionally fell apart when Eric left."

Madison sniffed loudly.

"I'm here to say that you need to take a long look at what you want in life. And more importantly, who you want in your life. You need to think about what kind of guy you're looking for and if Eric fits the bill."

Madison squirmed, hating that she knew everything her roommate said was true.

"Why can't life be easy? Why can't my knight in shining armor just appear and save me from all the hard things in life?"

April raised one eyebrow. "I mean, I don't want to be presumptuous, but isn't that kind of what Eric did when he pretended to be your boyfriend that night?"

Madison sunk lower and grabbed the bowl of popcorn. She needed all the carbs she could get right now.

*****

It was Monday evening, and Eric was headed into work. He'd slept most of the day, preparing himself for a night full of work. The problem was that he kept having dream after dream about Madison. Dreams of her yelling that she just wanted a pretend boyfriend for a night, not a real relationship.

Waking up had almost been a relief.

He looked through his phone, seeing he had two missed calls from a recruiter he often worked with.

He sighed. Obviously, his actions had been premature. Last week, he had called the recruiter, telling him to start keeping an eye out for any permanent computer tech positions in Denver. Eric knew it would probably take at least a month or two to find something worthwhile, but now it didn't matter. There'd be no point settling there.

As a matter of fact, he'd just avoid Colorado altogether until his feelings for Madison mellowed out.

He scrolled through his text messages. He saw one from April. Intrigued, he opened it up. It was short and sweet.

What the heck do you think you're doing?

Eric didn't have to be a genius to know she referred to Madison. The question was, what did she mean? Did she think *he* had broken things off with Madison? Because, if anything, it was the other way around. He was just going along with what Madison clearly wanted.

He typed out a reply.

Well, I think I'm about to go take a shower before I go into work. How about yourself?

Her reply was swift.

Don't be a smart alec. What did you do to Madison?

I didn't do anything to her. I did exactly what was asked of me. I played the endearing pretend boyfriend, then got out of her life. Exactly what she wanted.

After a pause, her next reply came.

I think you misread the situation, because Madison sure didn't get what she wanted.

Eric waited for more, hoping April would explain further, but that was all he got. He considered asking, but he knew she had strong loyalties to Madison and probably wouldn't tell him anything else.

What did she mean *Madison didn't get what she wanted*? She'd been literally writing out ways to explain his absence at breakfast yesterday morning. If she'd wanted to get back together, why would she have been doing that?

And why would she have been playing so hard to get this weekend? Sure, she started to warm up a little bit at the end, but she never once gave off the impression that she was into him.

Well, besides the kiss. That had been another story.

But he couldn't put all his bets on her reaction to a simple kiss.

No, as miserable as he knew it would make him, he'd stick to his guns this time. He and Madison were done, and there was no going back. She would remain in his memory as a fun weekend fling and that was all.

He put down his phone and made his way into the bathroom, wishing he could drown his emotions in the hot water.

*****

Madison sat at lunch with a group of her coworkers. One of the biggest health chains in North America signed a partnership agreement with Sube over the weekend, and Dave decided to take everyone out to celebrate.

She put on a happy face despite the fact that she couldn't feel less like celebrating. Because as much as she tried to get him out of her mind, Eric kept sneaking back in.

Liz sat next to her, keeping up a constant chatter with everyone around them. Madison tried to stay engaged, but she spent most of the time pushing her food around her plate.

Toward the end of the lunch, Liz grew quiet next to her and gave Madison a light elbow.

"So, are you going to tell me what's wrong?"

Apparently, Madison's acting skills were still subpar. "Oh, nothing. I'm just…I'm just a little tired. That's all." She gave Liz a halfhearted smile, praying the woman would accept her explanation.

Liz squinted at her. "How is Ethan doing? Have you two recuperated from last weekend?"

Madison stalled for a second, considering whether she should lie. But now was as good of a time as any to start spreading the story that she and Eric had broken up. "Um, actually, Ethan and I aren't together anymore."

Liz's fork froze midair. "What?"

"I said Ethan and I aren't together anymore. We broke up after this weekend." Madison looked down quickly, wishing she could hide the flush creeping up her neck.

"Oh goodness, was this…has this been a long time coming? You two seemed so happy and perfect together." Liz set down her fork and gazed at Madison with furrowed eyebrows.

"We were. I mean…I guess you could say things have been a little tense lately." Madison fumbled for words. She tried to remember the story she had settled upon. "He just travels too much, and I can't deal with it anymore. He's very focused on his job right now, so we decided it was best we parted." There, that sounded like a plausible excuse, right?

Liz reached over and placed her hand on Madison's clenched ones. "Oh, honey, I'm so sorry. Breakups can be rough. Are you sure you're okay with this?"

For some reason, the contact of Liz's hand over hers made Madison's emotions swell to the surface. Her eyes began to flood with tears, and there was nothing she could do to stop it. "Um, yeah…" She grabbed a napkin and tried to casually dab at her face.

"Oh sure, honey, let's go to the bathroom, and I can help you." Liz's voice had suddenly grown loud, and Madison looked up in confusion. Liz no longer looked at her, though. Instead, she spoke to those seated near them. "Madison's contact keeps slipping. I'm going to go help her fix it in the bathroom. We'll be right back."

She stood, bringing Madison up with her. Madison couldn't remember the last time she'd ever been so grateful to someone.

They walked to the bathroom with a steady gait, Liz's firm arm supporting Madison the whole way.

When they finally reached inside, Liz released her and walked to the paper towel dispenser. She tore off a large piece and soaked it in the sink.

"Here, wipe your eyes with this. The cold should help reduce any puffiness."

"Thanks." Madison sniffed and brought the paper towel up to her face. Liz was right; the coolness did soothe her weepy eyes.

"All right," Liz's quiet but determined voice said. "You don't have to tell me anything you don't want to, but you might feel better if you get it all out. What's going on?"

Madison stared at her, the flood of tears blurring her vision again. "I don't know, Liz. I don't know what I want anymore. To be honest, Ethan and I weren't as serious as I claimed we were. If anything, we were just...beginning our relationship with each other."

Liz stared at her, saying nothing.

Madison continued. "Anyway, things got rocky before the retreat this weekend, however, the time we spent together on Saturday made me think we could turn things around. But by Sunday, they were just back to how they had been." She pressed her lips together. "He doesn't really have feelings for me. I was just a fling for him, nothing more."

Liz sat silent a moment before responding. "You know, Dave and I weren't always friends before we got married."

Madison looked up, surprised by the turn in conversation. "You weren't?"

Liz shook her head, seeming lost in thought. "No, you could almost say we were enemies. You see, we worked for the sales department in the same company. Dave and I were basically direct competitors. We were always in a battle to see who could be the top performer." Liz looked at her hands as she talked, fiddling with the bracelets on her wrist. "In my mind, I viewed Dave as a cutthroat, brash businessman who felt he could brown-nose his way to the top."

A smile slowly appeared on her face. "Then, one day, Dave invited me to lunch. I was pretty sure he had an ulterior motive to it. But surprisingly, we had a great time together—more than great. We began to meet outside of work here and there, sporadically at first, but soon it got more consistent. In my head, though, we could have never been a thing. I had already defined who Dave was in my mind. I had put him in a box, and I was too stubborn to think I could've been wrong about him."

She looked at Madison who listened intently.

"It wasn't until he finally called me out on it that I realized how unfair I'd been. He asked if I would ever see him as anything other than my competitor. He told me he was willing to walk away from the job if that was what it took to prove that he didn't care about the position as much as he cared about me. It was then that I started seeing him in a new light. I started seeing him for who he actually was instead of the person I had decided he was. And here we are, thirty-two years later, and I haven't once regretted that decision to swallow my pride."

She reached forward and took Madison's hands, squeezing them lightly. "I'm not saying you are the same as I was all those years ago. Maybe you don't have impressions of Ethan you're holding onto. But if you do,"—Liz looked deeply into Madison's eyes—"perhaps you should consider giving him a second chance. Consider letting *him* define who he is instead of doing it for him."

The tears Madison had finally controlled came back in full force. Liz was right. She had created a set of expectations for Eric all along. Before she even met him, she'd assumed he was going to be a computer nerd that would be just as likely to embarrass her as save her at the company dinner.

Even now, after he'd shown up time and time again to help her, she doubted who he was. She kept assuming the worst and waited for him to fulfill her doubts.

When she really thought about it, what had he done wrong? Really nothing. He'd never broken his word or done anything he hadn't said he would. She'd known all along he was going back to work; it wasn't like he suddenly jumped ship. Even at the charity weekend, his sudden indifference shouldn't have been that surprising. She hadn't been overly warm and friendly herself.

"Thanks, Liz. I think I needed to hear this," Madison said, mopping up the last of her tears.

Liz rubbed her arm with a hint of a smile on her face. "Most importantly, make sure you do what's best for you. If that's letting Ethan go, then let him go. But if that's swallowing your pride,"—Liz paused and shrugged her shoulders—"then maybe that's what you need to do."

Madison nodded, letting Liz's words really sink in. "If you don't mind making an excuse for me, I think I'm going to head back to the office early. I don't know if I have any energy to socialize again."

"Don't worry, I got you covered. You go take care of yourself, and we'll chat later."

Liz turned and walked out of the bathroom door. Madison watched it swing shut behind her.

Taking a deep breath, she faced herself in the mirror. She knew what she needed to do. The question was, did she have the guts to do it?

Chapter 14

Eric had just stepped out of his apartment when his phone started ringing. Well, technically, it was the apartment the company had rented out for him for the month.

He looked down to see his sister's name flashing across the screen. They hadn't talked since her last text.

"Hello," he said, simultaneously reaching for the keys in his pocket.

"Hey, Eric, how's it going?"

He locked his door then hurried down the steps to the parking lot. "I'm doing fine, thanks." He paused, wondering what she could be calling about. "How about you?"

"Good, nothing too crazy to report."

He waited again, expecting her to lead the conversation. He finally added, "Well, that's nice. How's work been?"

"Oh, you know, just the usual. Lots of classes. Lots of training sessions. How is work for you?"

"Same old. Lots of coding. Lots of late nights."

There was another bout of silence as he looked for the silver SUV he was renting for the month. Impatience finally getting at him, he asked, "Alright, sis, what's the real reason you're calling me on a random Wednesday at two in the afternoon? I know it's not to ask how my day is going."

"Well, I love you too, Eric, and it's lovely to hear your voice as well."

Her slightly clipped tone made him chuckle out loud.

Ignoring his laughter, she continued. "Besides the obvious fact that I'm a loving sister who wanted to check on you, I did have a second purpose in calling. I need your address."

"My address?"

"Yes, I would like to know where you currently reside. Usually, it comes in the form of numbers and a street name."

Eric was pretty sure April's sarcasm was one of her best qualities. "I know what an address is, missy. I'm just curious why you need mine. Are you sending me a care package? If so, I am partial to home-baked chocolate chip cookies."

"I'll make a note of that, but no, I'm not sending you a care package. You left a shirt here last time you stayed, and I wanted to mail it back to you."

Eric thought for a second, trying to remember if he'd been missing any of his shirts. "Really? Are you sure it's mine? What does it look like?"

"Oh, you know, it's just a basic T-shirt..." April's tone lifted to an abnormally high pitch. "I'm pretty sure it was gray or something like that."

For the life of him, Eric couldn't recall any gray T-shirts he'd been missing. He didn't have a vast wardrobe, so it was quite easy to account for them all.

"I mean, I appreciate the gesture, but I'm pretty sure—"

April cut him off. "Anyway, that's what I called about. You think you could just text it to me?"

"Um, sure?"

"Great! So everything is going good?"

"Yeah, I guess everything's fine over—"

"Awesome. Okay, well, I'll probably get this in the mail, so expect something on your doorstep in a couple of days." She was clearly ready to get off the phone.

"Alright, um, take care."

"Love you, bye."

"Love you," he said as he heard the phone click off.

Well, that was weird. Eric was almost certain he wasn't missing a gray T-shirt. And more importantly, why had it taken April almost two weeks to realize he'd left a shirt at her house? From what he'd seen, she and Madison kept a pretty clean place. It was all very strange, but he shrugged it off. April always was a quirky one.

He typed out his address and sent it over.

It was only about two in the afternoon, meaning he should have still been sleeping, but he'd woken up around noon and had been awake ever since. He figured he might as well go get something to eat. Working the midnight shift didn't give him many eating options. His choices usually wavered between the twenty-four hour Taco Bell or a gas station. Neither one of them very appealing after about a week.

He pulled up in front of a local Thai place he'd found the first week he got there. He was hooked on their Pad Thai noodles. Ten minutes later, he carried a steaming styrofoam container to the most isolated table in the place.

Unfortunately, sitting next to him were two women who looked to be in their mid twenties and definitely single if their flirtatious glances said anything.

He tried to focus on his food, ignoring the giggling coming from their corner every few minutes.

Generally, this was a welcome opportunity for him. He was always game for a casual flirt with two attractive girls, but things had changed in the last two weeks. He was no longer interested in checking out other women. The idea of flirting with them seemed more like a chore than an enjoyment.

He kept telling himself he was just tired. He *had* been pulling extra-long hours the last few days to make up for his weekend trip. But he knew that wasn't it.

It was Madison. She was his first thought whenever he saw another woman. He wondered what she was doing, how work was going, and more importantly, he wondered if she ever thought about him.

Eric closed the container of noodles, not hungry anymore. He would just bring it to eat at work later.

Looking up, he caught the eye of one of the blondes sitting diagonally from him. She gave him a bright smile and a little wave. Impulsively, he contrasted her platinum-blonde waves to Madison's dark thick locks.

Almost groaning out loud, he shoved himself up and walked out of the place, only realizing once he reached his car what a jerk he probably looked like to the two women.

Oh well. What would having one more woman angry at him matter?

*****

"Alright, sister, I got the goods. We're in business."

"April, this isn't a heist. You just got your brother's address for me." Madison grinned as she spoke into the phone.

"You're not appreciating my undercover work, Madison. I had to be very sly to not make him suspicious."

"So he's not suspicious?"

Silence filled the other end. "Maybe."

"Ugh, you didn't tell him anything, did you?" Madison rapidly clicked the tip of her ballpoint pen on her desk.

"No. Oooobviously, I didn't tell him anything."

Madison could just imagine April waving her hands dramatically on the other end.

"He might've been a little confused about why I needed his address, was all."

"Alright, whatever. I guarantee, regardless of what you said, he won't be expecting me." Realizing how annoying the sound of her clicking pen probably was to her coworkers, she stopped.

"So, what are your plans anyway? Are you going to jump out of a cake on his doorstep? Oooh, maybe you should fill his car with balloons and a bunch of notes."

"April, I'm not asking him to prom."

"They always say big gestures are the way to a man's heart."

Madison leaned back in her chair and covered her eyes with her hand. "Nobody says that."

"Well, they should."

"To be honest, April, I don't know what I'm going to do when I get there. I haven't thought that far. This is a very 'by the seat of my pants' kind of decision." Madison sat back up in her chair, trying to ignore the sick feeling creeping in her stomach. "All I know is, I have a plane ticket to Boston that leaves tomorrow, and I have Eric's address. What exactly I'm going to do or say when I get there is still up in the air."

April didn't answer for a second.

"What are you going to do if he rejects you?" Her roommate's hesitant voice vocalized all of Madison's fears.

"I don't know." She was being honest when she said that. Who knew what she would do if Eric rejected her. She was putting all her eggs in one basket, putting her heart out on the line as Liz had suggested. But there was no guarantee that she would get her happily ever after. For all she knew, Eric could be well on his way to dating other girls. "All I know is, by doing this, I won't have any regrets."

"Well, when you get home tonight, I'll help you pick out your hottest outfit to wear. If nothing else, you'll stun him with your beauty. And if he does reject you,"—Madison smiled at the fierceness that entered April's voice—"I'm going to pound my brother into a pulp."

Madison just laughed. "Thanks, April. You're the best friend a girl could have."

They said goodbye, and Madison set the phone back on her desk. She looked at the computer screen, the half-finished project report that she'd been working on the last hour still in front of her.

Taking a deep breath, she scooted back toward her desk.

She didn't know what she would do when she arrived at Eric's doorstep. But she knew one thing: it was either going to heal her heart or break it.

*****

Eric stumbled into his apartment around 6 AM on Saturday morning. He'd had a problem getting his updates loaded to their server and stayed way too late fixing it last night—or technically, this morning.

Around 5:30, he'd successfully restarted the system, and exhaustion had overtaken him.

He dropped his bag in the entryway of his apartment and shuffled over to the couch. The apartment had come pre-furnished as most of his short-term leases did. He'd lucked out in this place. The main living area had a deep-seated leather couch in a neutral brown. As Eric had discovered from one too many late nights, it made an excellent bed.

The only thing that could've made it better might have been a nice lavender scent, he semi-conciously thought as he slumped across it that morning. Too tired to even take off his shoes, he left them on. He just needed a few hours of sleep, then he'd get cleaned up and make it all the way to his bed...

Three and a half hours later, he woke to a pounding noise. *Where is that coming from,* he groggily thought to himself.

He raised his head from the pillow, cursing the shaft of light coming through the blinds. Then it started up again, the hard pounding on wood. It wasn't until he heard someone speaking that he realized a person was knocking on his door.

"Eric! Are you in there? Please tell me someone's home," said the distinctly feminine voice.

Eric rolled over and put the pillow over his head. He was dreaming. He was still deep asleep and dreaming.

A final bang that sounded like a gunshot made him spring from the couch, scrambling to get his bearings.

"All right, all right, I'm coming!" he yelled at the door.

He yanked it open, not believing his eyes. There, in front of him, stood living proof of what he thought he'd heard: Madison, looking as radiant as ever, with the sun outlining her from behind like a lifesize halo.

"Madison?" He squinted against the sunlight, bringing his hand up to shade his eyes.

Her gaze roved up and down him. "Uh, hey, Eric. Sorry, is this a bad time?"

He suddenly realized what he must have looked like. Using one hand, he tried to smooth the wrinkled shirt he'd been wearing for almost twenty-four hours. At some point in his sleep, he must've kicked off one of his shoes, because he currently rocked one black sock and one gray sneaker. He gave up on his shirt and rubbed a hand over his face, feeling the vertical lines on his cheek from the throw pillow.

"Of course not." He opened the door wide and stepped back. "What brings you here on this fine Saturday morning...all the way from Colorado?" He tried to keep the shock out of his voice. What was Madison Hudson doing here on his doorstep? In Boston? How had she even found him?

"Um, I..." Madison stood in his doorway, suddenly frozen.

She seemed to scramble for something to say. Finally, she pulled her hands from behind her back, one of them holding out a brown paper sack. "I brought you breakfast."

Eric took the bag she offered, staring at her from the corner of his eye before looking down at the sack. Peering inside, what he saw made him want to burst out laughing. Slowly, he pulled out a cardboard box with a cartoonish drawing of a toaster pastry on it.

"You flew 2,000 miles to bring me Pop-Tarts?"

*****

Well, when he said it out loud like that, the gesture seemed kind of dumb. Madison was going for the cute, sentimental approach.

"Yeeeah," she said slowly. "Well, that's one of the reasons, I guess." She avoided eye contact and took a half step back. This wasn't turning out like she'd hoped. Eric was supposed to swing the door open, look at her with wide eyes of surprised adoration, then envelope her in a hug of happiness. Then, they'd pull apart and look into each other's eyes and—

"Madison?"

She blinked. Had he said something to her? "Uh, sorry, what?"

"I asked if you wanted to come inside." He opened the door a little wider, running a hand through his disheveled hair. She studied him, noticing the wrinkles in his clothes and the tired lines under his eyes.

She wanted to run from this trap she'd created for herself. But seeing the fatigue in his face somehow lowered her guard. "Yeah, thanks," she said as she walked past him. His familiar scent filled the air. It comforted her, reminding her that things were going to be okay. This was Eric.

She walked in, not sure if she should sit or stand for what she had to say.

"Here," Eric said, fluffing out the pillows on the couch, "have a seat."

Madison took his suggestion, perching on one edge of the leather sofa. She ran her hands down the dark jeans she wore. Her outfit had been very calculated. She had wanted to look good, but also not seem obvious about it. She had on fitted jeans along with a flowy teal top. Her auburn hair fell about her in loose waves. But no outfit or hair could have created enough confidence to take away the nerves pounding through her body.

Eric, on the other hand, seemed his same, comfortable self. He sat deep in the other side of the couch, his arm running along the back of it. He'd kept an eye on her the whole time she settled herself.

Madison wasn't sure what to do. Should she start with small talk or just get right to the chase?

Eric made the decision for her. "So...you doing some sightseeing here in Boston?"

The combination of his ridiculous comment and her nervousness gave way to a burst of laughter she couldn't control. Dropping her head to her lap, she filled the air with a giddy, borderline hysterical giggle. One that contained all the feelings she'd been bottling up the last few days.

When she finally got control of herself, wiping the stream of tears from her eyes, she saw Eric smiling back at her with a look of pure contentment.

"You really are a nerd, you know?" she said, biting back a grin.

"And proud of it," he said, pushing an imaginary set of glasses up his nose. He'd somehow managed to inch closer during her bout of laughter, his hand that had rested on the back of the couch now lightly brushing her shoulder.

Madison tried to ignore the tingling rushing through her at his touch.

Eric spoke again. "So, if you're not here to sightsee, are you going to tell me why you *are* here?"

The question hung in the air, the weight of it like a balloon just waiting to pop.

"Um, well..." Why was this so hard? Why was being vulnerable so hard? She stared at the wall ahead of her, her fingers itching to straighten the slightly crooked picture of a beach landscape. "I wanted to talk to you."

"I figured."

"Yes, well, I have some things I needed to say. In person." Madison took a deep breath and squared her shoulders so she faced him. She tried to recall the speech she had rehearsed probably a hundred times on the almost four-hour flight. But suddenly, she was staring into those blue eyes, and all her thoughts were paralyzed.

Eric shifted and took an exaggerated deep breath. "Alright, I'm ready whenever you are."

"Oh you…" Madison stood up in a rush, throwing her hands over her head. "Fine. I like you. That's it. That's why I flew 2,000 miles, and have lost endless nights of sleep, and have been on a mental roller coaster the last three weeks…because I *like* you."

She began pacing across the floor. "And it's ridiculous. It's ridiculous that someone I've known for less than a month—and realistically, have only spent like a week's worth of time with—has me feeling this way. I mean, I've dated lots of guys,"—she spun around, hand to her chest—"hordes of guys. And never once has any of them put me through the emotional turmoil you have."

She jabbed an accusatory finger at him. "Somehow, you have found your way inside my head, inside my heart! I'm at work, constantly thinking about how I can't wait to come home and tell you this funny story that happened, or complain about how something went wrong in the lab, and then I remember that you're not there." She stopped her pacing and planted her feet firmly in front of him.

He leaned forward, his arms resting on his knees. Madison knew she had his full attention, and if she was ever going to get this out, she had to do it now.

"I don't want you to just float out of my life now that our fake boyfriend/girlfriend arrangement thing is over. I don't want to go back to a life without your snarky comments that make me laugh uncontrollably. Or your terrible eating habits that I have to constantly comment on. Or the calm way you sit and listen to me blab about the meaningless drama I think is going on in my life." She began twisting her fingers through her hair. "I know this is nuts and probably out of the blue. You're probably wondering if I'm crazy. But I couldn't go on without telling you how I feel. I wanted you to know that you mean something to me. That if there's any chance your feelings mirror mine, I want us to try this. To figure out a way to make it work."

She paused, daring to glance at him before covering her eyes with her hands. "I'm blabbing. Oh my gosh, I'm blabbing. I don't know—"

Eric had stood up and reached out for her hands. He slowly lowered them from her face, interrupting her stuttering. "Mads, deep breaths." He pulled her toward him, his solid hands giving her a lifeline to hang on to. Despite her mental calm, though, her body tensed at his touch, something she had yearned for these last few weeks.

Madison gazed at him, his eyes seeming to search her own, almost as if they were looking for something. Had she said everything she meant to? What had she even said? Her mind felt even more jumbled as his hands released hers and trailed up her wrists to her elbows. One continued moving up until it cradled her cheek. Out of instinct, she leaned forward, the space between them nonexistent.

Their kiss began softly at first, but she didn't want softness anymore. She wanted a firm reassurance that his feelings echoed hers. Their kiss grew deeper, Eric's hands trailing through her hair, the tingling of his touch wrapping itself around her heart.

When they finally pulled back, they were both breathless.

Madison had to mentally tell herself to loosen the grip her fingers had on his shirt. Although this wasn't their first kiss, her racing mind knew this moment was a turning point for them.

Eric's gaze looked a little hazy as well, and he took a small step backwards, never letting go of her arms, though. "Alright, I'd better tell you a few things too," he finally said, pulling her back down to the couch.

She sat, this time fully relaxed next to him in contrast to her stance a few minutes ago. He interlocked their fingers, playing with hers through the moment of silence.

Breathing out a slow breath of air, he began. "So, I hate to say this, but I'm kind of a selfish person." He grinned but then got serious again. "I haven't really cared about anyone or anything else other than me for a while. But the last few weeks, things have changed that." He rubbed the back of one of her hands with his thumb. "It started at the charity dinner. I'm not going to try and be subtle; you about knocked me over when you walked out. I was pretty sure I'd never seen a more beautiful woman in my life."

Heat flashed across Madison's cheeks, but for once, she didn't notice because she was so absorbed in his story.

"I told myself that it was just going to be a one-night thing. That, after dinner, we'd go on with our separate lives. I decided to enjoy the evening to the fullest and leave it at that." Eric smiled down at their hands. "But I couldn't just leave it at that. By the end of the night, I was happier than I'd been in months. I had assumed it was because of the presentation about the charity work. I thought the opportunity to do some good in the world was what I'd been needing. That was why I suggested we go on the service retreat the following weekend."

He glanced at her, and Madison could see his throat bulge as he swallowed. "But I soon realized it hadn't been the thought of doing charity work that had made me feel so good. That had been a nice bonus, but the real cause had been you. Something about you made me so happy, in a way no one else ever has."

Now it was Madison who rubbed his hand lightly. She could see the tension leave his face with each word he said.

"If you didn't notice, I did everything in my power to hang out with you that next week. Leaving you early about killed me, but I knew it was the only way I'd be able to spend the following weekend with you."

"I bet you thought I was quite the drama queen that night before you left," Madison said sheepishly.

"No," he answered, "but I was a little confused. I wasn't sure exactly what I'd done wrong."

Madison just shook her head, not wanting to go back to those feelings. And most importantly, not wanting to break Eric's train of thought.

"Anyway, those weeks away from you were bad. It was like all the good feelings disappeared when you did. By the time I'd flown back for the retreat, I was determined to tell you I was looking for a permanent job in Colorado. No more of this jumping from place to place every month. I had finally realized that what I'd been missing out on in life had been the joy of caring about someone other than myself."

"You were going to move to Denver for me?" Shock ricocheted through Madison. Why had he not said something? Why had he left her so clueless and in the dark? But when she thought back to those days, she realized why. Because she had given him no indication she returned his feelings. If anything, he probably assumed the opposite by her juvenile behavior.

Eric nodded. "I was if I thought you wanted me to." He cocked his head. "You didn't give me the warmest reception, though. I tried melting your cold exterior for a while until I finally gave up."

Madison's head snapped up. "Wait a minute. What happened at the retreat?"

"What do you mean what happened?" Eric asked, his own head still tilted to the side.

"At the retreat." She bit her lip, not sure how much she should open up to him but assuming he should know it all. "I started out the weekend just wanting to get through it and move on. But you seemed so…"—she struggled to find the words—"flirtatious and open that first day. I decided maybe I'd been wrong and should give us a second try. But that second afternoon, you totally shut down on me. What happened?"

Eric raised one eyebrow at her. "Well, like I said, you sure weren't reciprocating my actions. And then when I saw your list in your notebook—"

"What list?"

"The list you were writing that morning at breakfast. The one about all the possible excuses you could use for why we were no longer together."

Madison's mind raced. List of excuses? She thought back to that morning. She'd been pouring her heart out into her notebook, and Eric had walked up to her. Then it hit her, what he spoke about. She *had* made a list of possible breakup ideas, but it definitely hadn't been that morning.

As a matter of fact, she had written that list before they'd even met, back when she was planning out the perfect fake-boyfriend scheme.

"First off, I was definitely not writing that list that morning. If you have to know,"—she itched to twirl a strand of her hair but didn't want to break the lock Eric had on her hands—"I was actually writing about my conflicting feelings for you and how I didn't want to risk getting my heart broken."

Eric opened his mouth to respond, but Madison cut in before he could.

"How—how did you see that, anyway?"

Eric raised one hand in defense. "When you knocked your water over at lunch, your purse flew off the table. Your notebook fell open to that page, so I assumed it was the one you'd been writing that morning." One corner of his mouth came up. "My inner ego took control, and thinking you were looking for ways to get rid of me just..." His words trailed off for a second. "It just made me want to escape the whole scenario."

Silence filled the room as they both processed this information.

"So, now what?" Madison asked, not having planned this far into her intervention.

Eric searched her face for a second before glancing at the coffee table. The corner of his mouth twitched slightly. "Well, I think the first thing we need to do is eat a well-balanced breakfast." He reached for the bag of Pop-Tarts and ripped them open. With a smile, she promptly turned down the first one he offered to her. "Well, then, I guess we'd better do some of that sight-seeing you came all the way here for."

"Oh you!" Madison said, reaching forward to slug him.

He caught her hand mid-air and, instead, used it to pull her toward him. Even though they'd technically kissed less than five minutes ago, his nearness still sent Madison's pulse racing. "Or we could just stay in, of course," he said, his lips brushing hers. "I mean, what are the sights of Boston to spending your day staring at me?"

This time, his mouth covered hers before she could protest. And Madison didn't mind one bit.

Chapter 15

(3 months later)

"Well, that was interesting," Madison said as the applause slowly died out.

"You know, I would never have categorized myself as an opera-lover before this," Eric responded, lightly massaging her shoulder, "but I could totally see more of these date nights in our future."

Madison rolled her eyes, leaning into the warmth of his hand. "Well, you'll probably be alone, because I'm pretty sure even charity couldn't get me to come to another one of these."

Eric laughed and looked around as the lights flooded the auditorium. "Oh, come on. It wasn't that bad. And think of all the kids in Mexico our contribution helped."

Madison gave him the side eye. "I feel wonderful for helping the children. But maybe next time, when you bid on an Oprah show, double check that it's actually Oprah."

"I think we need to work on your cultural side."

"Says the guy that has the collector's edition of every *Star Trek* episode ever made."

Eric placed a hand over his heart. "Never speak ill of *Star Trek*. In a hundred years from now, it will be honored as the masterpiece it is."

Madison just laughed as she reached down for her purse, her heels making no sound as they slid over the cushioned carpet.

Eric leaned over and put a hand over her arm. "Let's wait a second. I don't want to get caught in a parking lot jam."

His voice had a strange note to it. Madison noticed his eyes dart around the room, pointedly avoiding hers. "Okay...we can wait if you want." The group next to her had already left, but an elderly couple still sat next to Eric.

He removed his arm from behind her and tapped his fingers on his knee.

Madison studied him for a second. "Is everything all right?"

"Yeah, of course." Eric leaned back in a long stretch, but the stiff set to his shoulders made her question his relaxed gesture.

"Maybe you could get some of your new buddies from work to come to one of these with you. It'd be a great way to really bond with them all." She tried to mimic the blank look Eric was the master at.

"Huh, I'll have to bring it up with the guys tomorrow. They're a pretty cultured group, you know."

Madison couldn't hold in her snicker. Eric had been working at his new job for about a month now. He was the lead technician at a chain of manufacturing plants throughout the state, a prestigious position he deserved. Luckily, he had only good things to say so far, because Madison loved having him permanently close.

The couple that had been seated next to Eric finally filed down the row. The theater was almost empty. She glanced at him. "You think the parking lot has cleared enough by now?"

She was surprised to find him staring intently at her.

"Yeah...well, I really just wanted to be alone with you for a second, actually." Eric reached up and scratched the side of his head in a distracted way.

The air stilled a little, and Madison realized he no longer grinned in his usual way. He didn't look upset, but something clearly filled his mind. "Um, alright, what do you want to talk about?"

He reached out and gripped her hand. His usually warm palm was cool and borderline clammy.

"So...Madison."

Eric's formal tone was out of place and making her nervous. Was something wrong? She felt like things had been so amazing between them lately.

"About three months ago, I got these opera tickets at a charity dinner with the most amazing fake girlfriend I could have ever asked for."

One corner of her mouth lifted, tension leaving her shoulders and neck. "They did serve some pretty delicious steak that night..."

Eric just winked before getting serious again. "That night, as I sat next to you, all I could think was that this couldn't be real. I couldn't be sitting next to the most beautiful, most compelling woman I'd ever met and just be pretending to be her boyfriend. There was no way I was going to leave it at that. There was no way I was going to walk away from you and blow the chance of developing something real between us."

Madison smiled but didn't say anything. Where was he going with this? His grip on her hands tightened.

He looked down, a rare flush entering his face. "I...this is going to sound stupid, but when I bid on these tickets..." He gave a short laugh and looked at their entwined fingers.

Madison ducked her head so she could see his face. "You what?"

Eric closed his eyes, his breath slow and deep. "Madison, it's been a long time since I've ever felt this happy. The way I feel when I'm around you is something no other woman has managed to pull out of me." His eyes met hers. "I can't imagine not having you in my life. That week after that retreat, when I thought we had no chance, were some of the worst days of my life." He lifted her hand and kissed it. "I can't imagine ever doing it again."

He slipped one of his hands into his pocket and came out with a black object.

That was when everything froze.

What was he—was that? The questions she wanted to verbalize were streaming through her mind.

"What I told myself at that charity dinner was that I would find a way to convince you to marry me." One corner of his mouth lifted slightly as he lifted the object up.

The black velvet stood out in stark contrast to his light skin. He slowly cracked open the box, and a flash of sparkle hit Madison before she shifted her gaze to his. "Eric...are you?"

"Madison Hudson, you have captivated me since the second I laid eyes on you in your baggy T-shirt and holey jeans that first night."

"Don't remind me about—"

He held a hand up. "Then, you stunned me in a whole other way the next evening all done up. But no matter what you're wearing, you captivate me every time we're together." He lifted his other hand, and the single solitaire inside reflected at her. "Madison, would you make me the happiest man ever and be my wife?"

Madison sat in stunned silence, still not sure if this was all really happening. It wasn't until Eric leaned forward slightly that she realized how long she'd been sitting there.

"Yes!" she almost shrieked. "Oh my goodness, yes!"

She leaped at Eric, barely giving him enough time to pull the ring back to safety. His arms wrapped around her, holding her close. Their intense kisses eventually slowed until they rested with their foreheads touching.

"I can't believe I'm going to be Mrs. Madison Hudson," Madison whispered.

"I know. I can't believe I'm going to marry a nutritionist," Eric whispered back.

Madison giggled, pure happiness radiating from her.

"I'm going to have to keep a secret stock of Pop-Tarts somewhere, you know," he said, his voice still an intimate tone.

"I'll have you loving vegetables before you know it," she answered.

Eric leaned close again, his lips brushing hers. "If I get to be with you the rest of my life, it's worth it."

THE END

Before You Go:

Interested in the love lives of Madison's brothers Ryan and Mason? Don't miss out on their hilarious mishaps! Grab book 1 (A Temporary Marriage) and book 3 (A Temporary Engagement) of this series on Amazon!

*****

Note From the Author: Reviews are gold to me! If you've enjoyed this book, I'd love if you'd consider rating it and reviewing it on www.Amazon.com!

*****

To hear about my latest books first, sign up for my exclusive New Release Mailing List here: www.summerdowell.weebly.com

Manufactured by Amazon.ca
Bolton, ON